The Sla

The Jennifer Hunter Mysteries

By: Kacey Gene

For My Ya-Yas: The biggest mischief makers of all

Chapter One

Christmas Craft Chaos

Jennifer Hunter, or Miss Hunter as she's called by the second graders she teaches, always hears the screams first. And today, it is the scream of Lauren Bruso that grabs her attention.

Jennifer is a small woman -- reaching only 5'1" -- and she's round in places that let her second graders easily rest their heads on her lap or against her legs, and they feel comforted by her soft arms when she hugs them. She has deep brown hair that flows in soft waves to the middle of her back, and her hair always smells like cloves. Yet, it's her straight nose, green eyes, and caring -- although firm -- voice that give her the calm authority she needs on a daily basis.

"Hayden, honey, I'll be right back," she says.

Hayden is eight years old; he has dark, poofy hair and a face that looks exactly like Elvis Presley. He's attached to Jennifer at the hip, but since he's focused on his crafting, which he told Jennifer involves "macaroni and the baby Jesus," she can leave him to his pasta and settle the dispute that's now increasing in volume.

Jennifer's actually relieved to have a break from watching a baby's face be constructed out of macaroni. It is a terrifying sight.

By the time Jennifer gets to the crime scene, Lauren's tears have turned into blind rage. That rage is directed at Colin Majcina, whose eyes are as mischievous as his smile, which is as crooked as a hook.

Squatting down, Jennifer puts her hand on Colin's and Lauren's shoulders.

"He glued it," Lauren cries. "He glued my hair."

Quickly eyeing Lauren's cornsilk dark brown strands, which look like they've been dipped in marshmallow at the ends, Jennifer turns her full focus toward Colin.

"Colin," she says, looking straight into his nervous brown eyes, "tell me what happened."

Jennifer is used to having conversations like this. She's been teaching second grade for eight years, so she's seen it all -- boys who dipped their hands in honey so they'd be better at playing catch, girls who braided their hair into the hair of their best friend and then couldn't get apart, and the one boy every year who is the bug collector. This year that bug collector is Trey Johnson. In fact, he's currently making cockroach ornaments for his craft project.

Jennifer is sure his mother, Janet, will love getting that surprise when she opens the present from him.

"I didn't do it," Colin quickly says.

"I didn't ask if you did it," Jennifer says, "I asked for you to tell me what happened."

Colin is stumped. This is the trick Jennifer uses with kids and with adults. She doesn't ask for opinions; she asks for facts.

"I might have had glue on my hands," Colin confesses, now looking straight into Jennifer's eyes.

"And then what happened?" Jennifer asks, her voice always loving. Always promising that the confessor can tell her anything.

"And then I might have wiped my hands in Lauren's hair." Colin's eyes move over to Lauren, whose arms are crossed and lips are pursed.

"Colin, who got hurt in this situation?" Jennifer asks, knowing that it's her job to get these little ones to take responsibility for their actions.

"Lauren got hurt."

"Then I think you know what to do."

Colin turns straight toward Lauren, who is still dead-eyeing him like she's mentally plotting her retaliation. "I'm sorry, Lauren. I think your hair is really pretty."

And with one compliment, Lauren's icy stance shatters. "It's okay," Lauren says, uncrossing her arms with a shrug. And then she shyly smiles and says, "You think my hair is pretty?"

Jennifer can't help but internally laugh as she grabs Lauren's hand and says, "Let's go wash that pretty hair out in the sink."

Surprisingly, the rest of craft time continues without a hitch. By the end of it, there are 22 holiday crafts -- ranging from the cockroach ornament and the baby Jesus macaroni figurine to a cotton ball snowman without a face and a three-legged reindeer made from pipe cleaners.

Jennifer looks at the clock. There are only seven minutes left until the final bell. Seven minutes left until Christmas break. Seven minutes left until Jennifer can have two weeks full of sleeping in, crafting all day, and total relaxation. She's already fantasizing about the peppermint ginger tea she has at home and the tree skirt crochet pattern she hasn't even started yet. With the cold Wisconsin air already greying the sky this afternoon, she can't wait to get home, start a fire, put on her favorite Christmas album, and get crafting.

"Okay, kids," she says, "everyone gather round. We're going to read one story before I send you off for Christmas break."

The kids circle up as Jennifer pulls a book from the bookshelf that lines the side of the classroom wall. She snuggles down onto the soft carpet squares where the kids sit cross-legged with their elbows on their knees, waiting for her to take them to an imaginary place.

But before she can even crack the book's spine, Gabby has her hand in the air. Gabby has dozens of braids with bows at the ends, she loves to use large vocabulary words, and with every new activity, Gabby has at least two questions.

"Yes, Gabby?" Jennifer asks.

"I was curious as to who the gentlemen at the door is."

Jennifer's heart skips, and she immediately panics that it's Matt Kealy. He's the fourth-grade teacher, and just this morning in the office he caught Jennifer off guard with a question she never would have expected. He asked if she'd like to get a drink with him over the break.

Stunned and in a hurry, she gave a friendly, "That sounds great," but when Matt's face lit up, she realized that she might have agreed to something she didn't realize she was agreeing to. A date.

But it's not Matt at the door. It's Jake -- the 6'3", dark-haired, strong, and always trailed with trouble, Jake. He's standing in her classroom door with a vulnerable and somewhat apologetic look that Jennifer knows all too well.

"Is he your boyfriend?" Gabby asks, which initiates giggles from the entire class.

Jake's serious face cracks into one of slight embarrassment as Gabby and the other kids continue to giggle. Jennifer even thinks she spots a blush lightly come to his cheeks and a small smile attempt to grip his mouth.

But Jake is not her boyfriend. And Jennifer knows there's only one reason that he's here: there's a dead body somewhere surrounded by unanswered questions, and Jake needs her help.

Chapter Two

The Face in the Bowl of Pudding

The house is made of large grey and brown stones, like it fell from the pages of an old fable book. It's small, with only two criss cross windows, and the front entrance is cone shaped without any windows. *It's like a mini castle,* Jennifer thinks.

The house is about a ten minute drive from Main Street downtown, which is where Jennifer lives. Their town, Middlebridge, isn't necessarily big by any standards -- every corner of it can be reached in under twenty minutes. It's the kind of town where familiar faces smile at Jennifer in the grocery store, her doctor remembers when she had pneumonia in fourth grade, the woman who owns the local diner knows Jennifer's order, and it's also the kind of place where a secret transforms into gossip within a matter of hours.

But Middlebridge is also a big enough town that Jennifer can look at the house in front of her and not know who lives there.

Jennifer and Jake duck under the CAUTION tape, and Jennifer glides her hand across the large wooden front door that's propped open. The entryway hall, which is long, narrow, and made fully of stone, is also pitch black and a bit musty. Jennifer imagines that living among walls and floors of rock lends itself to a bit of must. Jake clicks on his flashlight, but even that beam of light doesn't do much to light the way.

"Oh," Jennifer yelps as one of the stones wiggles below her and sends her off balance. Without realizing it, she grabs onto Jake's arm, which barely flinches against her grip.

"You might as well just keep hold of my arm," Jake says, carefully watching each one of his steps. "It only gets worse from here."

"I'm perfectly capable of walking," Jennifer says, but the moment she gets the last prideful word out, another stone wiggles, causing her to topple and brace herself against the wall.

"Perfectly capable, huh?" Jake says just under his breath, but Jennifer hears every word, and she sees the smile he thinks the unlit hallway hides.

"Oh, shut up," Jennifer playfully says, brushing off her grey pea coat. She pulls at the bottom of her cream cable-knit sweater and smooths her black skirt. When she feels her foot wobble beneath her again, she lets out a defeated, "fine," and grabs onto Jake's arm.

It's not that she's upset Jake came to her for help. They've been friends since second grade, and she's helped him out dozens of times before. And Jake always respects her rule: he can only ask for her help when she's on holiday -- seeing as there's no way she could balance crime solving and second graders. And they both know she can't resist trailing a crime until it's finally solved. She just wasn't expecting him to show up the exact second her Christmas break started.

She keeps thinking about all the presents she needs to make, and she can already hear the words of her demanding, always-in-competition-sister-in-law, Julie: *Oh, I see you used regular strawberries for the jam this year. I only ever buy organic. I'll send you an article about it.*

Julie buys organic, she only shops at stores that sell free-trade items, she's vegan, and she has evangelical opinions about all of those choices. Jennifer likes Julie, it's just that Julie is four months pregnant, and Jennifer promised a crocheted stocking for the baby-to-be. Julie will expect it to be perfect. And Jennifer doesn't want to disappoint her -- or deal with the judgment and comments that come from that disappointment -- but she knows that for something to be perfect, it requires time and focus. And she only has four days until Christmas.

But all of those thoughts drain from Jennifer's mind when she and Jake turn the corner and she sees the victim. His white hair contrasts against the dark wooden table, which is where his face lies, in a bowl of something brown and liquified.

"No. No. No. This is a possible crime scene. She cannot be here," Captain Sharb barks. He comes waddling over to Jennifer and Jake, standing directly in front of Jennifer and blocking her view of the body.

Jennifer has been helping Jake out with cases since the day Jake started at the Middlebridge station. As Jake tells her each time he comes back to her for help, "No one's brain can piece together clues like your brain." So Jake never got a partner, and the other officers at Middlebridge station eventually accepted that Jake and Jennifer were going to periodically work together. It helps that Jennifer also brings her famous chocolate muffins into the station every weekend. That sweetens the other officers.

Except Captain Sharb.

"You know she can help," Jake says, challenging Sharb.

But Sharb is a Captain and Jake is a Lieutenant, so Sharb easily says, "I don't care if she's already solved this crime. I want her out of here."

Jennifer has never understood why Captain Sharb hates her so much. He's built like a Russian Doll -- as if someone grabbed his middle, pulled from all sides, and then never balanced out the top and bottom of him -- and his face is always red, like he's either on the brink of yelling or just finished yelling.

"Sharb, let her through."

Jennifer would recognize that voice anywhere. It's the Police Chief Jefferson Hollow. Of course, she doesn't know him as "Police Chief Jefferson Hollow;" she knows him as Jake's dad.

"How you doing, sweetie?" Jefferson asks as Jennifer strolls right past Sharb. Jefferson envelops her in a hug and gives her a kiss on the cheek before he holds her by the shoulders out in front of him. "Pretty as a picture," he says, shaking his head. "When is my knucklehead of a son going to come to his senses and marry you? I love it when my J&J are together."

Now it's Jennifer who blushes. Jake's dad has been calling them "J&J" since grade school and questioning their relationship since high school, even though they've explained millions of times that they're "just friends," and happy to be.

"Do you think we could at least pretend to be professional, Police Chief Hollow?" Jake asks, circling the table where the victim lies.

That table is in the middle of the kitchen, which looks like it traveled back in time. There are copper pots and dried bunches of herbs hanging from the dark, wooden beams that grid along the kitchen ceiling. The cabinets are made of chipped and distressed wood, and the stove sits by itself, taking up almost half of the wall. The stove has six doors on the front of it, and when Jennifer gets closer to it, she sees that it's the kind of stove that has to be lit with a match.

"Victim's name is Fred Gailey," Jefferson Hollow says.

"That name sounds so familiar," Jake says, reaching into his memory but coming up empty-handed.

"It's the father's name in *Miracle on 34th Street*," Jennifer says, having seen that movie hundreds of times. But she's not focused on the victim's name; her eyes are occupied with the stock pot, which could almost be called a cauldron due to its size, on the stove. It's bubbled over with the same brown sauce that's in the bowl on the table. It releases a stench that overrides the musty smell in the air.

It's a combination of hazelnut and milk with just a small hint of brewed coffee.

"Pudding," Jennifer says, returning her eyes to the brown liquid splattered across the table where the victim is. "He's in a bowl of pudding."

"Well, look who cracked the case," Sharb sarcastically says. "We know it's pudding, but what this man was eating when he died isn't why we're here."

Jennifer is about to explain what she's already pieced together, and what these other officers have completely overlooked, but before she does that, she crouches down and gazes into the cloudy blue eyes of the victim. They're the most circular eyes she's ever seen, almost like a fish's eye. And that's when she has her moment -- the moment when she thinks about how this man is possibly someone's father, someone's husband, someone's friend, or someone's smile on a bad day. She lets the sadness that he's gone overwhelm her and then she makes him a promise -- a promise that she'll find out what happened to him.

"But he didn't make that pudding," Jennifer says, knowing that if he did, it would be on his clothes or smeared on his hands or forearms in some way. But his hands, which are splayed against the table like the arms of a cactus, are meticulously clean, not one crescent moon of darkness under his fingernails.

"Well, this cabinet would disagree with you," Sharb says, opening the cabinet that's above to the white farmhouse sink.

Jennifer can barely believe what she sees. There are pudding boxes lined up next to each other, stacked on top of each other, and shoved into every corner of the cabinet.

"They're all empty," Jake says, walking by Jennifer. "All the pudding has been used."

"Why would he keep all the boxes?" Jennifer silently asks herself.

"Not quite the detective you thought you were," Sharb says, but Jennifer ignores his snide remark. Instead, she eyes the trash can, which is almost completely empty. More importantly, there isn't one discarded box of the pudding mix in the trash, which further confirms her notion that Fred Gailey was put in a bowl of pudding, but not a bowl of pudding he made.

"That does seem like a lot of pudding for one man," Jake adds. The two police officers who have remained silent on the sides, scribble down notes and one of them moves to the pot of pudding and photographs it.

"I still don't think we can throw out that maybe this man simply died and fell into his pudding. Sometimes a death is as simple as that," Sharb says, closing the cabinet.

"He was boiled in this pudding," Jennifer says, keeping her focus on Fred's dead face and seeing that there are red marks under the side of his eye. They're somewhat hidden by the crusted brown pudding, but the longer she looks at his face, the more red marks she sees. "Look at this," she says to Jake, who squats down next to her.

"She's right," Jake says. "There are red marks on his face." He motions for the police officers to come and take more photographs.

"Are you saying this man was murdered by pudding boil?" Sharb asks, with judgment coating each of his words.

"Did you check his chest?" Jennifer asks, ignoring Sharb. She doesn't mean to be rude, it's just that the pieces of this crime link and lock together in her mind like a trail, and she has to follow it.

"We didn't want to touch the body until you got here," Jake says, quietly. "But we did a visual scan and there's nothing. No marks. No signs of struggle."

"Check his chest."

Jake first looks at Jefferson, who not only nods his head in approval but joins Jake on the floor. They duck walk so their heads are just under the table and then they get on all fours to flash their lights up at the man's chest. The other surrounding officers point their recording devices and cameras at this change in action. Sharb crosses his arms and shakes his head in annoyance.

The flashlights illuminate the shadows under the table.

"Nothing," Jefferson says, but he gives it a few more seconds before he stands up. "No blood. No wounds. Nothing."

"Like I said," Sharb arrogantly adds.

"Maybe Sharb is right on this one. I mean, who are we to judge how much a man loves pudding?" Jefferson lightly asks. "And if he died just after making the pudding, then that would mean he fell into a hot bowl of pudding, and that would explain the red marks."

"But his face," Jake says, still crouching under the table, "his face doesn't look right."

"It's in a bowl of pudding," Sharb quips, but he takes a step back when Jefferson sends him a glare of warning.

"Look under his sweater," Jennifer says, feeling her hands shake. She agrees with Jake, something here isn't right. She can feel it.

Jefferson and Jake put on their gloves, and it takes their pristine focus to not jostle the body too much as they pull at the neck of Fred's grey, loose-knit sweater. Luckily, it's an old sweater, so the neck easily opens and Jake aims his flashlight down into the tunnel it makes.

"What is that?" Jake asks, his eyes growing big.

"Is that a…" Jefferson pauses as he reangles his flashlight, "a part of a plant?" he asks, equally confused and intrigued.

"It's a sprig of holly," Jennifer says, without even having to see what they're looking at.

"Well, I'll be…" Jefferson says, looking up at Jennifer proudly.

Sharb sees this look of admiration, and it causes his face to redden like a boiled beet.

"There's no way a stick of holly, or whatever it's called, killed this man. I mean look at that thing." Sharb gestures to the small sprig, which the police team carefully holds between their tweezers and then place in an evidence bag.

"For once, I agree with Sharb," Jennifer says, but somewhat absentmindedly. "It was made to look like the holly and pudding killed this man, but that's not it."

"We need to get the holly tested," Sharb says.

"Already on it," Jake says, and his eyes and fingers become occupied with his phone. He texts the lab with specific instructions about what tests to run on the holly and the pudding sample that are coming in.

Turning from the victim's body, Jennifer scans the rest of the house, which consists of a small family room and two doors off of it, which Jennifer assumes are a bedroom and bathroom. She takes two steps down into the sunken family room and focuses on the back wall. It has an old stove fireplace, but even more importantly, it has an entire wall of books. And not just any books, but old books, collector's items.

"May I?" Jennifer asks Jefferson as she feels herself being drawn to the book shelf.

He gives her a nod and then turns to give instructions to the two police officers who are staring at the holly like it's going to spontaneously come to life and break into a song and dance.

Jennifer starts on the right side of the book shelf, the end of the alphabet, and she makes her way past first editions of Edith Wharton and cracked and dusty spines of John Steinbeck. Tracing the books with her eyes and then her finger, which floats in front of the books as she reads the authors' names, she finally gets to the D's.

There is a matching set of books, just as she suspected. They're bound in a green leather, they have gold writing for the titles, and the pages, which she can see if she stands on her tiptoes, are thick and also edged in gold. These books are by Charles Dickens, and as she reads the titles from the end, starting with a *Tale of Two Cities*, she passes over *Oliver Twist, Nicholas Nickleby, Little Dorrit, Hard Times, Great Expectations, David Copperfield, Bleak House,* and it ends with *Barnaby Rudge.* But there's one book missing, and that book is the answer to this crime.

Chapter Three

A Christmas Carol Clue

"*A Christmas Carol?*" Jake asks. "What do you mean *A Christmas Carol* is our answer?"

After the last police car pulls out of the Fred Gailey's driveway, Jake puts Jennifer's blue SmartCar into gear and heads toward her apartment. Now she's glad that she kept this theory to herself at the crime scene. If Jake is skeptical, then Sharb would have torn her idea apart, and she's not ready to have her theory shredded before she's fully stitched it together. It's exactly like her crochet projects -- at first they look like a big old mess of knots, and then suddenly, those knots become a stocking, a sweater, a basket, or a baby's blanket that brings comfort for days to come. Her projects just need time and attention to become something, just like this theory.

"Did you not pay attention at all in eighth grade English?" Jennifer asks, but she can't hide her smile when she looks over at Jake. She always makes him drive when she's with him, not only so she can multitask but also because she takes such pleasure in seeing his 6'3" body shoved into her tiny car.

"In Mrs. Bollegar's class? No. You couldn't pay me to stay awake in that class."

"And you probably still got an A," Jennifer says, looking at him with suspicious eyes.

Jake smiles a proud grin and says, "I sure did."

That's because Jake got A's in all his classes; yet, he didn't even like school. He couldn't wait to graduate from high school and from college, and when he was done, he had no desire to ever return. Jennifer is the exact opposite. Even after she graduated, she put herself right back in the classroom, but this time as the teacher.

"Well, if you had paid attention, you'd know that this crime scene is an actual scene from *A Christmas Carol.*"

Jake looks at her skeptically. "I may not remember the book, but I watched the movie. The version with Scrooge McDuck. And I don't remember a murder or a man with his face in pudding."

"It's not that exactly," Jennifer says, scrolling through her phone and searching for the direct quote. "Here it is," she says, having found the passage. "And I quote from the book: *If I could work my will, every idiot who goes about with 'Merry Christmas' on*

his lips should be boiled with his own pudding, and buried with a
stake of holly through his heart.

"It really says that?" Jakes asks, leaning over and eyeing the passage that scrolls across Jennifer's phone.

"But why would someone reconstruct Scrooge's words into a scene and then steal the book the words came from?" Jennifer asks out loud to herself.

"We don't know that the book was stolen," Jake says. He holds his finger in the air as a warning.

"Jake," Jennifer says with a give-me-a-break look, "the man had almost every Dickens novel ever written, so it doesn't make sense that he wouldn't have what is one of Dickens' most *famous* novels. Plus, those books came in a set."

"Okay, so what if *A Christmas Carol* wasn't in the set he bought?" Jake retorts back. "And I don't know a ton about books, but I know that the older things are, the more expensive they are. If *A Christmas Carol* is so famous then maybe Fred Gailey couldn't afford an antique version of it."

"Good point," Jennifer says as her memory shifts back to Fred's house. It was humble in every other way -- no expensive furnishings, small in size, decorated for function rather than style --

so by all visual accounts, Fred isn't wealthy, or if he is, he definitely isn't showy about it.

"Hey, did you get any--" but before Jennifer can get another word out, she lurches forward, almost hitting the windshield with her head.

Jake's fingers grip the steering wheel so tightly that his knuckles pop up like gumdrops. Jennifer looks in front of them to see what they hit, but then she sees Jake's eyes fixated on the rearview mirror. Jennifer whips her head around.

There's a black car with tinted windows right on their tail, which for a SmartCar means it's almost in their backseat. Jennifer wonders if that black car is going to keep pushing into them until it breaks through her back door, but the car slams on its brakes and falls feet and then yards behind them. But then, the black car's engine rips into a roar, and it speeds straight down the road toward them.

"Jake, he's coming back," Jennifer yells, watching the car get closer and closer. "Jake," she yells again, feeling her panic spike with every inch this black car closes between them. She imagines it all unfold -- the black car hits them from behind, they spin out of control, her car acrobatically flips until smashing into a tree, and the whole time she and Jake are flopping inside the car until...darkness.

She hates herself for it, but all she can imagine is the disappointed faces of her family. Not only will none of them get their handmade Christmas presents, which they are all expecting, but her death will put a damper on the holiday. Her mother will never forgive her for that.

Jennifer squeezes her eyes shut, readying herself for the impact that she knows will come in seconds, but rather than being thrust forward from behind, Jennifer smashes against her seat as Jake floors the gas pedal. With not much weight to carry, the SmartCar zips into action, making the possible killer-hit from the black car simply tap their bumper.

"Hold on," Jake says, leaning into the steering wheel with his eyes hyper-focused. Jennifer turns her head to the back windshield and sees the black car fall back again, but this time it's not speeding back up. It's going in reverse.

"He's reversing," Jennifer says.

"Get the plates."

Jennifer squints. She picks out a P, E, L, Z, N, K, L.

"Pelznkle," Jennifer says out loud, immediately second guessing the

letters now that the car is even further in the distance. The P could be a B, making the plates "Belznkl." She curses being almost thirty and now needing glasses to see far distances.

But, then, all of her vision jumps as her body bounces and bobs in her seat. Suddenly, she and her car are not only up on a sidewalk, but Jake is parking her car in someone's yard -- right between the inflatable snow globe and the blow-up Santa lawn decorations.

With the reflexes of a stealthy cat, Jake quickly asks, "Are you okay?" to which Jennifer nods. But before she can ask the same of him, he's unbuckled himself, unholstered his gun, and jumped out of the car. He takes off running straight for the black car, which Jennifer sees is now a spot in the distance.

But that doesn't stop Jake, whose black boots echo against the sidewalk.

Rolling her already stiff neck, Jennifer gets out of the car, but she feels like she steps into a winter wonderland rather than a front yard. The Christmas carol "Let it Snow" is playing all around her, there is a snow machine blowing pieces of white confetti into the air -- as well as in her hair, in her mouth, and all over her grey coat -- and the house where her car is "parked" has every window dotted with a red-bowed wreath. The house itself is covered in white lights, and its bay window frames a gargantuan Christmas tree, which twinkles for everyone who looks in the window.

And three children.

There are three children with their noses, hands, and eyes pressed against the glass of that bay window. Their mouths and eyes are open in awe at the car that's parked on their lawn. They're currently speechless, but Jennifer knows that will be short-lived.

Moving behind the car, Jennifer surveys the damage. Her bumper is dented, one of her back lights is cracked while the other one is completely shattered, and the blue paint on her car is scratched.

"Not terrible," Jennifer says, rubbing her neck. She hears Jake's footsteps as she looks closer at the damage to her car. Jake is out of breath when he gets to her, and his eyes are wide with worry.

"You sure you're okay?" he asks, turning her around, checking her for wounds, and looking at the top of her head.

"Jake," Jennifer says, brushing away his hands, which are fingering through her chestnut brown hair like a monkey grooming another monkey. "Jake," she says again, finally getting his attention.

"I'm totally okay. What about you?" she asks, but then she sees it. He has a small cut right above his eyebrow.

"You're bleeding," she says.

Jake quickly feels where she's looking, wipes the blood away and says, "I'm fine."

"No. You're bleeding," Jennifer says. "Come on, I'll drive you to my place and get you bandaged."

"I can drive," Jake says, instinctively. He always drives, and he doesn't want that changing just because he almost got them killed in a car chase and is bleeding from the head.

"You need to call in the plates," Jennifer says, knowing that refocusing Jake is the best way to get him to comply. "And I have a rule. No driving while bleeding."

Jake doesn't argue any further. The two of them walk back to her car, but just as they are about to get in, a very tense and very pursed voice says, "Excuse me. Do you want to tell me what you're doing on my lawn?"

The owner of the house is standing between the herd of reindeer that are lined up on his front porch. The three children that had their faces pressed against the window earlier are now circled behind the man, trying to peer around his legs to see the action.

The man's arms are crossed, his face is uncompromising, and his warning of, "I"m going to call the police," sparks an ironic smile from Jake.

"I'll take care of this," Jake says to Jennifer, realizing that this man can't see his uniform thanks to the dark sky. "Go ahead and start the car," he tells Jennifer, and she knows that he'll talk his way out of this. Jake can talk his way out of everything and charm any and every person he meets. Except one.

My mother, Jennifer thinks, and the panic she felt when the black car was about to run them off the road is nothing compared to the fear she feels now. Jennifer frantically checks her watch.

6:11 PM.

Her mom will call her at exactly 6:30 PM, just as she does every night. And if there's one person that no one makes wait, it's Jennifer's mother.

Chapter Four

Ring-a-Ding-Ding

Jake is at least five paces behind Jennifer, who attempts to move down her tan-carpeted hallway as silently as possible. She doesn't want her neighbor, Mrs. Muscolino, coming out.

It's not that she doesn't like Mrs. Muscolino; it's just that Mrs. Muscolino is always dialed to hyper-negative. She's eighty-seven years old, with a hunched back, a cane for walking, and terrible cataracts in both eyes. Whenever she talks to Jennifer, it's about the terrible state of the world, her latest ailment or pain, and how she doesn't trust this or that person because they're on their phones too much.

Jennifer listens, and she completely understands how hard it must be to see the world you used to know change so much. But then Mrs. Muscolino goes to a much darker place. A place where she pretends to ask Jennifer questions, but her questions are really more like judgments than anything else.

You're still not married? Not even a boyfriend?

You wore that outfit around elementary school kids?

Another day without makeup, huh?

You're cooking in again tonight?

Jennifer is convinced that even if she came home one day in a pristine outfit with a full face of tasteful make-up and a husband hanging off her arm (carrying Mrs. Muscolino's favorite meal -- pesto pasta with parmesan) that Mrs. Muscolino would still find some fault in it. And the weirdest part is, Mrs. Muscolino lives with her sister, Tina, and her sister is the sweetest peach in the world. Jennifer loves running into Tina Muscolino, who at the age of eighty-one acts at least twenty years younger.

Then Jennifer hears it -- the ringing she was trying to beat.

"Shoot," Jennifer says, sprinting down the hallway. Her phone rings a second time. She fumbles with her keys, but finally her door gives way and she throws herself on the counter and grabs the phone. "Hello? Mom? Hello?"

"Yes, dear. What is wrong? You sound frantic and out of breath."

Jennifer's mother is never frantic or out of breath. Everything she does is scheduled, controlled, perfectly calm, and if not, then someone else deals with it. Her mother does not do messy.

Jennifer takes a deep breath and swallows, even though her throat is completely dry.

"No. No. Nothing is wrong. I just wanted to get to the phone."

Jennifer thinks about how much easier this would be if her mother would just call her cell phone, but her mother refuses to use "plebeian communication devices," as she calls them. Her mother only uses the landline phone that's in the study of her Chicago penthouse apartment. And, she only makes calls from 6:00 PM until 7:30 PM. Anyone who wants to talk with her, must abide by those hours -- all other hours of the day are reserved for her staff to take messages and for her to be phone free.

"You didn't answer until the third ring. Where were you?"

Jake walks through the door and slides Jennifer out of her coat before taking off his own and hanging them both up on the rack next to her front door.

"I was out."

Her mother knows nothing about what Jennifer does with Jake, and that's the way she wants to keep it.

"With whom?" Her mother's voice sounds tighter than usual. She typically has a voice of perfect sophistication, like the sound of warm tea being stirred.

"I was with Jake."

Silence.

"Mother?" Jennifer asks. She knows that her mother dislikes Jake, or more specifically, she dislikes that Jake is in Jennifer's life. Her mother has no interest in hearing about people like Jake -- people who work, people who don't hobnob at parties and talk about art, opera, and orchestras. Jennifer's mother, Eleanor, is the one person Jake has never been able to charismatically win over. Jennifer knows this bothers him, even if he doesn't admit it.

"Do you have everything in order to be here for Christmas?" her mother asks, completely changing the subject.

Her mother always does this. Whenever they move into a conversation her mother doesn't want to have, she simply steps right out of it and begins another. That conversational hopscotch is especially reserved for any mention of Jake, Jennifer's job, Jennifer's choice to not live in Chicago, and...Jennifer's father.

"Yes. I have my bus ticket, and I'll be there by 7:00 PM on Christmas Eve. In time for church." Jennifer frantically calculates her tasks and time in her head. She has exactly three days to get eight jars of jam made, three batches of cookies baked, and all the presents made, wrapped, and ready for Christmas Eve night.

"Bus ticket?" her mom asks, aghast. "What do you mean *bus* ticket?" She says the word "bus" like it's covered in dung beetles. "I sent you a plane ticket that gets you in by 10 AM on Christmas Eve. The driver --"

"David," Jennifer interrupts, not liking that her mom often refers to people by their jobs rather than their names.

"Yes, David is going to pick you up so you have enough time to change."

"Change for what?" Jennifer asks.

"We have reservations for holiday tea, dear. At The Pavilion at the Langham. It has all been arranged. The ladies are counting on you being there."

Jennifer cradles the phone in her neck and throws her hands up in frustration, which elicits a sympathetic and understanding look from Jake. He knows all about the tea ladies who bring their small dogs to afternoon tea, eat finger sandwiches, and gossip rather than talk. In fact, there's not much Jake doesn't know about. He and Jennifer tell each other everything, well...with one exception.

In all the years they've known each other, they've never mentioned the word "girlfriend" or "boyfriend" to one another, even though both of them have had partners and gone on many dates. Jennifer will even keep her accidental date with Matt Kealy underwraps until after it's over, since talking about has-beens is completely acceptable in their friendship. But, in every other way, she and Jake are there for each other. They take care of each other.

Then Jennifer sees the blood that's still on Jake's forehead. She holds her hand over the phone's receiver and whispers, "Alcohol and bandages are in the linen closet by the bathroom. Bring them out here."

Jake nods before pantomiming a dainty tea drinker with his pinky pointed up. Jennifer can't hold in her giggles.

"Jennifer, I do not call you so you can converse with someone else," her mother says sharply.

"Sorry, mom. Sorry. I'm listening."

"Then it's settled. You will be on that plane. The driver will pick you up. And you will be at holiday tea, just like every other year."

"Yes, mother." Jennifer says, slumping down on one of the stools she has lining her kitchen island. She rests her elbows on the cold white and grey granite, hating that she doesn't have any fight left in her. She wants to argue. She wants to give her case for her right to ride the bus and arrive when she wants.

"It's all settled, then. I will call you tomorrow night. Love you, dear."

And just like that, the line goes dead. Jennifer hangs up the phone just as Jake reemerges with alcohol, cotton balls, and bandages. Jennifer directs him to the stool next to her, and without saying anything about the conversation she just had, she gets to cleaning his wound.

It's not a deep cut, but Jennifer is meticulous in her cleaning. Jake never winces as she puts the alcohol on the cut or pushes on the bandage once it's applied.

"So," he says as Jennifer clears the pop-up medical station. "What did Queen Majesty Hunter of the Gold Coast have to say?"

"The usual," Jennifer says, not wanting to talk about the fact that she caved into her mother once again. Jake despises that interactions with her family always put Jennifer in a bad mood. A distant mood. Although, at least her mother calls her.

Jennifer hasn't heard from her father in over ten years. Jake knows she'll never admit it, but he's convinced that's why she moved back here after college. Sure, she grew up here, but she left when she was thirteen -- when her parents finally got that divorce they always threatened. Her dad stayed here; her mom went back to her family money in Chicago and the expectations that went with it. Jennifer teetered between the two worlds, spending summers and holidays here and the rest of her time on the Gold Coast.

Jake wishes she knew that she could talk to him about her mom, even if her mother does hate him. He's about to tell her this exact thing when his phone goes off. Pulling it out of his pocket, he sees a message from his dad.

"They ran the plates," Jake says, and the mood in the room changes from sullen to electrifying.

"Which did they run? The P-version or the B-version?" Jennifer asks, relieved to have a different focus.

"Both. They said the B-version isn't registered anywhere."

"Which doesn't mean they don't exist."

"Right," Jake says, knowing that forged plates on a killer's car are about as rare as mosquitos in the summer. "The P-version has a match, and the guy lives here in town. The plates belong to a Matthew Kealy."

Jennifer almost drops the alcohol and the bandages as her mind translates Jake's words -- the license plate of the person who just tried to kill them belongs to the guy she unintentionally accepted a date from just this afternoon.

Chapter Five

Candlelight Crafts

Jennifer always sets her alarm for 6:00 AM, but there's really no reason to. No matter what time she goes to bed, she always wakes up right around 5:30 in the morning. Not that she's complaining. It's her favorite time of the day, when the sun hasn't stretched itself into her life, and everyone else is still asleep, including Jake, who is currently camped out on the couch in her main room.

She tried to offer him her bed, but he wouldn't hear of it, and as he said last night, "If you're booking drinks with killers there's no way I'm letting you sleep here by yourself."

"In that case," she said, throwing him an apron, "you're helping me make this jam."

It wasn't until they had all the strawberries chopped, the lemons juiced, and the sugar measured that Jennifer brought up Matt Kealy again.

"It just doesn't fit," she said. "Matt Kealy makes Rice Krispie treats every Friday for the teaching staff, and maniac drivers and Rice Krispie treat makers just don't go together."

Jake met her justification for Matt's innocence with a skeptical look, but he let the subject drop. Instead, he focused on boiling and sanitizing jars while Jennifer cooked down the strawberries into a sweet pile of mush.

In the end, they made nine jars of fresh strawberry jam (eight for friends and family and one for them). By the end of their jamming session, her entire kitchen was splattered in strawberry stickiness, and even this morning she can still smell the remnants of crushed berries mixed with lemon and sugar in the air. She feels a bit more at ease knowing that one of her Christmas tasks is now checked off the list. Only three more projects to go. And a murder to solve.

Pulling out her crochet pattern for Julie's baby-to-be's stocking, Jennifer lights the balsam and fir candles she has lining her bedroom windows. She loves to crochet by candle light while the sun comes up. Her grandma on her dad's side was the one who taught Jennifer to crochet, and in those candle-lit sunrises, she feels like her grandma is there with her in some way.

When Jennifer gets the last candle lit, she sees a giant snowflake glide past her window. Then another. And then another. She goes over to the glass door that leads to her balcony, opens it, and takes in a deep breath of the cutting air. Even though she immediately starts shivering, she stays outside and looks at the Christmas trees that light up the windows across the way. Jennifer wonders if there's someone on the other side looking at her tree. This year she went all out, making Jake help her lug the 8-foot tree all the way down her hall and into her apartment.

She has it positioned at the back of the main room, so it's the first thing she sees when she walks in the door -- its dark green branches, white lights, and handmade ornaments that were passed down from her great grandmother to her grandmother to her mother and then to her. Jennifer loves these kinds of traditions, and as she steps out on her balcony and looks up at the dark sky that still has some residual stars in it, she's reminded of another tradition.

She opens her mouth and catches a snowflake on her tongue. Her dad taught her that, and he used to do it with her every first snow fall.

She thinks about how the snowflakes taste exactly the same as they did back then, even though so much else has changed.

As the wind whips into her bedroom, Jennifer closes the door, snuggles herself into the thick, navy blanket she has folded at the end of her bed, and crawls beneath her white, puffy duvet. Pulling her crimson and grey yarn right next to her, she takes her crochet hook and begins the chain for the stocking. When she gets to 43 chains she starts to single crochet into each back loop, and her mind threads together the pieces of Fred Gailey's murder.

Even though none of the lab results are back yet, Jennifer knows that Fred was murdered, no matter what Sharb argues. Her mind wanders into questions about why someone would recreate that quote from *A Christmas Carol*. Does that mean the person loves or hates Christmas? For that matter, did Fred Gailey love or hate Christmas?

There wasn't much in his house that would point to him being a Christmas lover -- there wasn't a tree, a wreath, or any scents of cinnamon or pine. But there was a ridiculous amount of pudding, and something in Fred's eyes makes Jennifer feel like he loved Christmas. She can't explain it, but the most important clues are almost always the inexplicable kind.

And why would the killer take the book?

Jennifer hears Jake's warning in her head: *we don't know the killer stole the book.*

She crochets to the end of her row, chains a single loop, and goes back down another row of single crochets while she replays everything from yesterday evening. She needs to prove that the book was taken, but how can she do that?

"The book dealer," she says, almost missing a stitch with her epiphany. Those old Dickens novels aren't just something Fred would have picked up in a random store. They must have gone through a book dealer or a specialty book shop, so maybe the novels have a stamp or some type of sticker in them. If she contacts the seller of the Dickens books, she can find out if *A Christmas Carol* was in the set, and it's possible the book dealer will even know Fred Gailey. I's not exactly an easy name to forget, and she can't imagine that the people who buy antique books are a large group.

Excited by her new trail, she casts off her crocheting and runs to her bedroom door. She opens it and is about to yell her idea to Jake, but then she sees him peacefully sleeping in the yellow glow of her Christmas tree lights. The red and grey blanket she crocheted last year in Chicago is draped across him, and his hair is sticking out every which way on the pillow.

He looks so childlike and cute that Jennifer can't disturb him. Plus, she hardly ever gets to see him like this. He always has an air of police and crime business around him, but this Jake -- the one that interlocks his fingers when he sleeps -- is the one she remembers from when she was little. It's her best friend, who currently needs his sleep.

She convinces herself that her idea will be just as exciting when he wakes up. She thinks about the croissants she has in the freezer and the strawberry jam that's resting on her countertop. They'll have that and a steaming pot of ginger tea for their breakfast.

Bam.

Jennifer almost lurches out of her skin when the sound slams against her window.

Bam.

The sound comes again, this time waking up a very confused Jake, who looks surprisingly at Jennifer.

"What was that?" Jake asks, his voice groggy but alert. "And why are you watching me sleep?" he asks, sitting up.

"I wasn't watching you sleep," Jennifer says defensively, even though she was doing exactly that. But the chill coming from her bones concerns her more than that small lie. "Did a bird hit my window?" Jennifer asks, but it's still too dark for birds to be flying.

Bam.

"There it is again," she says, now realizing that this is no longer a random sound. Something is being thrown at her window. But she's on the eighth floor of her building. No one could throw something that high up.

Jake gets up from the couch, his white t-shirt askew and his plaid boxers hitting him mid-thigh.

"Stay back," he says, guiding her to the wall where she has her fireplace. He moves toward the window.

Bam. Bam.

The hits are more frequent now. Jennifer's eyes adjust to the darkness, and she sees that whatever is getting flung at her windows is oozing down the glass.

Bam. Bam. Bam.

One after another comes, and now Jennifer's heart is leaping and pounding. Whoever is doing this knows where she lives.

More than that, if they don't stop, Jennifer isn't sure how long her windows can hold out.

But then the attack abruptly stops. Her windows are covered in a substance that's as dark as mud.

"What is it?" Jennifer asks Jake, who's standing at the brick column that separates her windows. He angles his view, but without more light, he can't determine what's seeping down the glass.

"I'm not sure, but I think they've--"

Pound. Pound. Pound.

Jennifer jumps back so quickly that she knocks over the nativity scene she has displayed on her fireplace mantle. The little lambs drop and go rolling across the floor.

Pound. Pound. Pound.

Someone is knocking on her front door, and the fist is pounding harder and harder. Jennifer can't help but hear how similar it sounds to the attack on her windows. As she looks at her front door, she can't help but think that the killer is on the other side of it and coming for her.

Chapter Six

Nosy Neighbors

Jennifer turns her eyes on Jake, who holds a finger to his lips -- miming for her to remain silent. He tiptoes over to his pile of clothes next to the couch and pulls out his gun. Like a cat on the prowl, he walks past Jennifer mouthing for her to "stay here," as he moves toward the door.

But there's no way she can stand idly by -- next to her red and white stockings that hang from the garland she has snaked around her now disheveled nativity scene -- while Jake approaches her front door with a gun. She needs to know who's at the door. She needs to know who's after her.

So, ignoring his command, Jennifer trails in the silence of Jake's footsteps.

When they get to the door, Jake looks back at Jennifer with anger and annoyance across his face, but it's not because she ignored his request for her to stay put. "You don't have a peep hole?" he whispers, his voice as tense as a whisper can get.

"It didn't come with the apartment," she whispers back, defensively. "And a 'peep hole' wasn't high on my to-do list." Jennifer explains.

"I can hear your voice, Jennifer Hunter." It's the person on the other side of the door. The voice is crackly, grumpy, and Jennifer immediately recognizes it as Mrs. Muscolino's voice. Her tense shoulders fall, and Jennifer confidently moves toward the chain lock to unfasten it.

Jake grabs her hand before she can unlatch anything. "What are you doing?" he asks, still keeping his voice hushed.

"It's my neighbor Mrs. Muscolino."

"So?" Jake says, pulling Jennifer behind him. "She could still have something to do with this."

Jennifer shakes her head as Jake keeps the chain latched, hides his gun from sight, and opens the door just a crack.

"You mind telling me why--" but Mrs. Muscolino doesn't finish her sentence. "Oh, you're not Jennifer," she says, and Jennifer hears a change in Mrs. Muscolino's voice. It's not grumbling and guttural like it is when she talks to Jennifer; instead, Mrs. Muscolino is talking like each of her words is being delivered by angels.

"No, I'm Jennifer's friend," Jake says, seeing what Jennifer already knew -- that there's no way this perturbed, eighty-seven-year-old woman could have anything to do with whatever got launched at Jennifer's windows. "Do you mind waiting just a moment so I can unchain the door?"

"Of course not," Mrs. Muscolino coyly says.

Closing the door, Jake holds out his gun to Jennifer and says, "hide this," but Jennifer crosses her arms in protest. He knows she hates guns. He knows that she won't touch guns. With an apologetic look he quickly hides it in the Santa cookie jar Jennifer has in the middle of her kitchen island.

When he opens the door Jennifer takes her place next to him.

"Good morning, Mrs. Muscolino," Jennifer says. Mrs. Muscolino throws Jennifer a side glance with pursed lips and slanted eyes, but then her lips and face soften when she turns her attention back on Jake.

"Seems that someone was playing a Christmas prank this morning," Jake says. "It woke us up as well. I can't apologize enough for the noise." And then he flashes his smile -- his big, dimple-creating smile that makes every woman Jake has ever used it on swoon into admiration.

"Oh, it's no problem. I just wish I knew Jennifer had company." She throws Jennifer a disapproving and menacing glare when she says this. "I wouldn't have come over here in this state if I'd known there was such a man here." Mrs. Muscolino apprehensively touches the curlers she has tightly rolled in her hair and adjusts her cotton nightgown that has sleeping cows on it.

"I'm not sure you could look more beautiful," Jake says with a smile. "Although, I'm always happy to be proven wrong by a woman."

Jennifer almost gags right then and there, but then she sees the effect Jake's words have on Mrs. Muscolino. She's beaming -- like high noon sun in August that's reflecting off a shiny surface and blinds your eyes kind of beaming.

"Okay," Jennifer says, grabbing the edge of the door, "we're sorry about the noise, Mrs. Muscolino, and we'll get to the bottom of what happened."

Before Mrs. Muscolino can protest and lure Jake into more compliments, Jennifer shuts the door, only to hear Mrs. Muscolino say, "With manners like that, she'll never keep that man."

Jennifer shakes her fists at the door, and Jake breaks into laughter.

"You should be ashamed of yourself," Jennifer says. "Flirting with a vulnerable eighty-seven year old."

"Don't get jealous," Jake says with a sly smile. "She does have better nightwear than you, but--"

Jennifer playfully hits his arm before he can get another word out. She turns back to look at her windows, and somehow, the sun has sneakily peeked through the dark sky and turned it a light shade of crystal pink. It's just enough light to illuminate the brown goop that is starting to cake and freeze on her windows.

Jake, seeing that her attention has focused back on the attack, walks over to the windows with her. They look at the brown substance like it's a piece of art in a museum -- investigating it from far away, up close, and then from different angles.

"Come on," Jake says, nodding to her bedroom. "Whoever did this can't hide under night anymore."

They go into her room and step out onto her balcony. Jennifer wraps her arms around herself when the cold air hits against her bare legs and arms. She wishes she could wear pants and long sleeves to bed, but at night she heats up like the inside of a cooked sweet potato, so full pajamas are basically an overheating death sentence. She learned this the hard way when she was six years old and begged her parents for footie pajamas. She got a pair for Christmas, immediately put them on, and she almost spontaneously combusted that same night. From then on, it's always been tank dresses for bed, which is proving to be worthless against this cold December air.

Jake leans over the edge of her balcony so he can get a better look at the outside of her windows. He realizes exactly what Jennifer put together earlier -- there's no way someone could have launched this substance from the ground.

He looks across the way at the other apartments, which reach to 10 floors and create a U-shape.

"Do you have binoculars?" he asks.

"I do," Jennifer says, running inside. Her bedroom has two closets, which most women would fill with shoes, dresses, and purses, but not Jennifer. Her smaller closet is dedicated to clothes and accessories, while her larger closet -- which she can stand in the middle of and spin around in with her arms out -- is dedicated to crafting.

She heads into that closet and walks past the white shelves on her right that hold overflowing baskets of yarn, her two sewing machines that her Aunt Jamie got her a few years back, past the jars full of crochet hooks, thread, and bobbins, and she touches the silk ribbon she just bought. It hangs on the wall with dozens of other ribbons.

In the back she has an antique dressmaker's dummy that holds different pieces of jewelry and scarves she's made. She loves the way the chunky red and cream scarf she crocheted last week, and that will be perfect for Valentine's Day, contrasts against the dark iron of the dummy. But her binoculars are on the other side of her closet -- the side with reams of wrapping paper anchored to the wall and shelves full of glue guns, fake flowers, buttons, beads, and dozens of books on everything from candle making and canning to flower arranging and decoupaging.

"There they are," Jennifer says, reaching up to the top shelf and grabbing the binoculars. Jennifer never uses these. Her dad gave them to her on her fifteenth birthday. That same night he told her to point them at the sky, and he directed her to a specific star.

"It's our star," he'd said.

He'd bought it for her. Named it after the two of them. And just when she was going to ask him, "Are you being serious?" he handed her the certificate. There it was in writing -- star number A2453 was now named "Sammy and Jennifer."

"This way we can always be together," he'd said, "no matter what."

Jennifer should have seen that little gift as a warning. A warning that her dad was going to disappear, which he did two years later -- the day she went to college. No more birthday cards, no more birthday phone calls, and no more communication at all.

By her junior year at the University of Iowa, and three years of silence from her dad, Jennifer stopped expecting anything. At first she asked Jake to have his dad investigate what happened to Sammy, but Jake talked her out of it. He said it would only hurt more.

So Jennifer swore she'd forget her dad, just like he'd forgotten her. She also swore she'd never stargaze again. Yet, she kept the binoculars.

Jennifer shakes those memories and the sadness that's spreading through her out of her mind and heads back to Jake. "That's the past," Jennifer tells herself as she closes her closet door. Through her bedroom windows she sees Jake eyeing something in his hand.

The second she steps back onto the balcony he says, "It's pudding. And it was launched in balloons," he says, holding up the hot pink shred of latex he is holding.

"Seriously?" Jennifer asks. "More pudding?"

"Yep," Jake says, taking the binoculars from her. He scans the apartments across the way, and Jennifer immediately worries that her neighbors are going to think they're a couple of perverts -- out at 6:30 in the morning and aiming binoculars at the apartments across from them.

But then Jake's scanning stops. He holds the binoculars steady and looks over at her.

"We found our launching pad," he says, gesturing for Jennifer to come look. She stands in front of him as he holds the binoculars steady. She feels the warmth coming from his body behind her, and she wants to snuggle into it, but then she looks through the binoculars and sees exactly what Jake saw.

The apartment one up and two over from hers has a giant hole cut out in the glass door leading to the balcony, and in that hole is a tube that looks perfect for launching small, circular objects.

"You know who lives there?" Jake asks.

"Of course not. I only learned the names of everyone on my floor this year."

"Well, get dressed," Jake says. "You're about to meet a new neighbor."

Chapter Seven

Marley's Ghost Returns

After dozens of unanswered knocks on the door of 9N, a stench that smells like burnt rubber emanating from the bottom of the door, and a warning of Jake saying, "We will break down the door if you don't answer," Jake tells Jennifer to step back.

He pulls out his billy club and strikes the door knob. It takes a few hits, but the brass knob eventually gives and falls to the floor. With a hole in the door, Jake pulls out the hook wire he has, fishes it through the hole, and unlatches the dead bolt. Luckily, this apartment owner doesn't use the chain on his door, so Jake easily pushes it open.

But Jennifer wishes that door never opened. At first, all she sees is the body. It's slumped over in a chair like a melted candy cane. But it's the smell that forces her to turn her head away and cover her nose.

"My God," Jake says, immediately pulling out his phone and calling for backup. He puts his hand on Jennifer's back. "Go wait outside," he says, but she refuses to leave. Then they both look toward the kitchen, which is the main culprit for the stench.

Just like at Fred's, there's a giant pot of pudding on the stove, but this batch is scorched, burnt, and blackened to a crisp, and it smells like burnt doll hair.

Jennifer, wanting to keep her distance from the body, watches Jake as he walks over to the victim and feels for a pulse. That's when Jennifer sees the chains criss-crossing across the victim's chest. Those chains anchor him against the chair and are the only thing stopping this man from folding over on himself.

"Anything?" Jennifer asks, reminding herself to breathe deeply and slowly.

Jake shakes his head. No pulse.

Jennifer has seen terrible crime scenes before, but something about this one rattles her. A big part of her wants to turn away, to run to her apartment and bake the cookies she needs to make and crochet the tree skirt and stockings she'd planned to focus all of her attention on before Jake showed up in her classroom. But then she reminds herself why she's here. She's here to catch the people that do this. To stop future crimes from ever happening. Cookies and stockings will have to wait.

She shakily steps to where Jake and the victim are, and that's when she sees the cuts. This man is not only chained to his chair, but he has cuts on his arms and all over his legs.

But superficial cuts won't kill a person, and Jennifer's heart pulls on her brain with the question she always wonders.

"Could we have saved him?" she asks Jake. Her words and her hands shake as she scans the victim's body for an obvious fatal mark, but it's all superficial wounds. *Was this man left to starve to death? Is that how he died?* she wonders.

Jennifer rubs her neck as her anxiety fizzles through her body. "If I would have woken you up earlier. Or if we would have discovered the launch pad earlier. Maybe we could have gotten here and saved his life," Jennifer says, her words frantically falling out of her. "Instead we wasted time talking to Mrs. Muscolino. We could have saved him, Jake. We could have saved him."

Jake pulls her into a hug and uses his soothing, deep voice and the facts to calm her.

"No, Jennifer, we couldn't have," he says, side-eyeing the man's body. The cuts on his arms and legs aren't red or fresh. Whomever did this might have killed this man last night or even the day before -- the same day they found Freg Gailey murdered.

"You promise we couldn't have saved him?" Jennifer asks, looking up at Jake but keeping her head pressed against his chest.

"You know I never lie to you," Jake says, and Jennifer sees his face change. Yes, he's concerned about her. Yes, he's trying to comfort her. But there's something else there. An unstated desire; something he wants to tell her and never has. And, he looks like he's on the edge of telling her, which completely unravels her.

She no longer wants her face that close to his, so she mumbles a soft apology for her reaction, pulls away, and turns toward the victim.

Jake, not wanting to live in the tension that just came into the room, gets closer to the body and has to cover his nose due to the stench that smells like hot garbage.

"What is that?" Jake asks, examining the burns closer. A few of them have a thick almost gooey substance in them. "It's like the killer cauterized the cuts, but with..." Jake pulls out the wire he used to unbolt the lock and pokes one of the wounds. He brings the gooey-coated end of the wire to his nose and sniffs.

"Let me guess," Jenifer says, eyeing the brown substance.

"Pudding," Jake says, confirming what Jennifer thought.

Jennifer plays out the scene in her mind and realizes that this man wasn't just killed, he was tortured.

"The killer wanted some kind of information from him," Jennifer says, knowing that where there are torture tactics there are almost always questions in need of answering. But what could this man know? He looks around the same age as Fred Gailey; he has white hair just like Fred; but while Fred was thin and gaunt, this man has a bulbous stomach and legs and arms as thick as tree trunks.

Jennifer sees that he's wearing a white cotton nightshirt. It's one of those old ones she's seen in movies about 19th-century England -- the kind that come down to the knees and look like they should be paired with a nightcap like in *'Twas The Night Before Christmas.*

"Look at this," Jake says, having moved behind the chair where the man is chained. Jennifer steps around the chair, and she can barely believe what she's seeing.

There's an old safe at the base of the chair, and it's the hub for all the chains that crisscross across the victim's chest. The safe has four legs, which are iron and look almost spider-like due to the way they curve out and have a sleek, oil color. Those legs prop up and hold the body of the safe, which looks to weigh at least 50 pounds. Jennifer and Jake crouch down to get a better look at it, and that's when they see the etchings. There are currency signs, sketchings of banks, and drawings of coins on it.

Those images, the safe itself, and the chains around the man finally link together in Jennifer's mind. "Why didn't I see it?" she asks, standing up and frantically looking for a bookshelf. But there isn't one book in the main room.

"See what?" Jake asks, following her gaze, which moves from one wall to the next and then to the next. Jennifer runs into the man's bedroom without a word, and Jake quickly follows behind.

"The books," Jennifer says. "We need to find the books."

"Jennifer, you aren't making any sense."

"It's *A Christmas Carol,*" she says. "The killer made the victim into Marley."

"Marley?" Jake asks,

"You didn't read the book last night, did you?" Jennifer says, pretending to be disappointed.

"Well, I planned to," Jake says, "But then I found out that my best friend made a date with a guy who possibly tried to kill us. My mind was occupied with things other than reading."

"Fair point," Jennifer says, instantly feeling awkward with the reference to Matt. She opens the victim's closet, hoping to see a shelf of books, but she's greeted with nothing but clothes and racks of shoes. "In *A Christmas Carol* Marley's ghost visits Scrooge to warn him of all the spirits that will come to him that night. When Marley arrives he's covered in chains and he's dragging a safe," Jennifer says, looking at Jake, who is as surprised as she is by these words.

As Jennifer pushes through this man's tweed coats and button-down shirts, she loses hope that there are any books in this closet. But then, she freezes. Right before her, hanging in the very back of this man's closet, is a puffy, velvety red Santa suit. And it's the nicest Santa suit she's ever seen. The velvet is plush, the white trim of the suit has silver strands woven through it, and the gleaming black belt is perfectly polished and carefully anchored around the hanger's neck.

"Oh-kay," she says, pulling out the suit for Jake to see.

"Wow. That's the fanciest Santa outfit I've ever seen," Jake says, taking the suit from Jennifer's hands. He looks at the front and the back of it as he concludes, "It looks like our John Doe was a really classy Santa somewhere."

Jennifer can feel that this suit and the information are important, but for right now, she has one mission: to find those Dickens books she knows are in this apartment.

The victim's apartment is the exact same layout as her apartment -- with the open kitchen that overlooks the main room, which is where the fireplace is. He has the same set of large windows on the back wall, so his bathroom and linen closet must be tucked in the hallway behind the kitchen, just like her place. That means this man will also have a second closet in his bedroom just like she does.

And just as she predicted, there's a door next to the closet she's standing in front of. But this closet doesn't just have a door knob. It has a padlock battening down the hatches.

"We need to get in that closet," Jennifer says, looking at Jake, who is turning the Santa suit and looking at every stitch. Jennifer switches her gaze to Jake's billy club, and that gets his attention.

"We really should wait for the other officers to get here. This is a crime scene, and we shouldn't tamper with anything else."

Jennifer knows he's right. She knows they should do the responsible thing and follow protocol, but she also knows that there's a murdered man in the next room. And even though Jake says they couldn't have saved him, Jennifer believes she could have. If they would have dug up more information on Fred then maybe it would have led them to this man before the killer got here. After all, both victims are around the same age, and their murders connect to the same Dickens novel. And Jennifer has no intention of being steps behind again. She's here to save lives, not follow protocol.

So she calmly moves toward Jake and says, "I know you're right," and when she sees that his guard is down and his focus is back on the snazzy Santa suit, she grabs the billy club from his belt, turns to the closet and attacks the padlock.

After three solid *whacks* the padlock drops to the ground.

"Remind me never to get on your bad side," Jake says, disapprovingly holding out his hand and requesting his club back.

Jennifer apologizes, hands it to him, and throws open the closet door.

"You've got to be kidding me," Jennifer says, when she sees towers and towers of pudding boxes. They reach from floor to ceiling, and they are the exact same brand and box --greyish white background with large print black letters -- as the ones in Fred's kitchen cabinet. And just like at Fred's they're empty.

"What is going on with this pudding?" Jake asks, but Jennifer can't even focus on his question because there in the back of the closet is the set of Dickens books that she was looking for. They're wrapped in red leather rather than green leather like the ones at Fred's house, but they have the exact same gold script and gold-edged pages.

Jennifer moves closer to them and reads the titles: *A Tale of Two Cities, Oliver Twist, Nicholas Nickleby, Little Dorrit, Hard Times, Great Expectations, David Copperfield, Bleak House,* and *Barnaby Rudge.*

The only one missing is *A Christmas Carol.*

65

Chapter Eight

Captain Sharb Gets Serious (Part I)

Captain Sharb has yelled before, but never quite like this. Jennifer has been "escorted" out to the hallway, and even though Jake and Sharb are in the victim's bedroom, she can hear Sharb's words as clear as glass.

Through all of Sharb's insults and profanities directed at Jake, Jennifer only hangs onto a few words: "irresponsible" and "unprofessional" and, worst of all, "probation." She props her boot-covered foot against the wall and looks over at the police officer who is standing guard outside apartment 9N. He returns her look, but while her look is kind and apologetic, his is annoyed. It's only 7:15 in the morning, and Jennifer presumes he's not so happy about the work wake-up call he received thanks to her and Jake.

"McCleerey," Sharb yells. His footsteps stomp against the hardwood floors as he gets closer to them in the hallway. "Get in here, McCleerey. I want you to photograph this entire scene even though it's already been polluted with amatuer ignorance."

"Yes, Captain," the officer says, and Jennifer plots how she can sneak back into the apartment now that Sharb will most likely have it on lockdown. The second she discovered the books in the victim's closet is the second that Sharb and his team came storming into the place. She barely understood what was happening before two police officers, on Sharb's command, grabbed her by the arms and pulled her out into the hallway.

"And you," Sharb says, now fully in the hallway and directing his angry glare straight at Jennifer. His face is blistering red, and there is sweat beading all around his thinning hair line. "I want you out of here."

"If I could just come in and take a look at one--"

"Out," Sharb yells, his words are so forceful that Jennifer actually takes a step back. "Or I will have you arrested for obstruction of justice."

"Alright, Captain," Jake says, a strength in his voice that's only covered up by the respect he knows he needs to give Sharb right now. "I'll get her out of here."

"And don't *you* think you're coming back either. I mean it, Jake. You're not on this case. Not after what you and girl-wonder pulled."

Jake doesn't say a word, even though Jennifer looks up at him with eyes that beg for an explanation.

"Is he serious?" she asks once they turn the corner and head down the next hallway.

When Jake remains silent and keeps his hand locked around her upper arm, Jennifer fears the worst. Did she get Jake kicked off a case? Did she get him in trouble in a permanent way?

Guilt walks alongside her as she scolds herself for breaking into the victim's closet. If she would have waited, then eventually Sharb and the other officers would have opened the door and all this drama would have been avoided.

But she couldn't wait, and she wonders how Sharb expects her to be in a crime scene that has a trail of clues and not follow them. That's like expecting a starving person to gratefully chew on some ice even though there's a feast on a table in front of them.

"Jake, talk to me. Please," Jennifer says when they reach the elevator.

Only when the elevator doors close does he let go of her arm and finally open his mouth. "Sorry," he says. "I didn't know how long Sharb was going to watch me, so I had to keep up the act."

"Are you really off that case?"

Jake lets out a smug sigh. "He wishes," Jake says, pushing the button for floor 8. "Sharb is mad, but he'll cool down. I guarantee he'll be asking for my help by tomorrow." Jake runs his hands through his hair and leans against the elevator wall. "*Polluted with amatuer ignorance,*" he says, shaking his head. "I would never compromise a crime scene. Those guys would have done exactly what we did. Sharb is just mad because we were there first, and he hates anything that has him being the receiver, rather than the giver, of information."

Sensing that Jake is aggravated but not particularly worried about this situation with Sharb, Jennifer playfully asks, "Are you saying he wants to give rather than receive?" She looks over at Jake. "In that case, Sharb has the true Christmas spirit in him."

Jake meets her gaze and right before he breaks into laughter, he pulls her into him like a loving brother. Jennifer half expects him to give her a noogie when he says, "You're ridiculous, and I love it," but she really hopes he doesn't. She has her long, chestnut hair anchored in a ponytail, and she really doesn't want to have to redo it. Jake plops a friendly kiss on the top of her head and then lets her go.

Relief comes over Jennifer -- not only because she's noogie-free but also because they're out of that apartment. There was a frantic energy that seemed to absorb through her skin when she was in there, and she has this strange feeling that if she stayed there too long, it would have become permanent.

But, she once again missed the opportunity that she wishes she would have taken last night at Fred's house -- to look inside the books. Because what if both sets of books came from the same seller? Or what if there is a clue or a message or something inside the books? Then she could really start moving and piecing together these killings, which she's positive are linked.

"I know that look," Jake says just as the elevator doors open to her floor. "What are you plotting?"

"Fred's case and this case aren't connected in Sharb's mind, right? I mean, you didn't tell him any of the Marley business did you?"

"I didn't have a chance," Jake says, getting to her door and unlocking it. He holds it open for her. "He walked in and immediately started yelling."

"So Sharb doesn't connect this murder with Fred's murder?"

Jake quizzically pushes his eyebrows together as they move into Jennifer's apartment. He leans against her kitchen island. "No. At least not yet. But once he sees the pudding and the books, he's going to link them together," Jake says.

"Well, then," Jennifer says, grabbing their coats from the rack next to her door. She reaches into her coat pocket and asks, "Do you want to drive or shall I?" She jingles her car keys in the air.

"You want to go back to Fred's?"

"I want to go back to Fred's," she says matter-of-factly and loving that Jake can always keep up with her mental acrobats.

"And you expect to drive your busted, tinker-toy car?"

"Hey, it's not a tinker-toy," Jennifer says, defensively, but Jake's right; it's really in no shape to drive around town. "I was thinking we could pick your car up and drop mine off at the shop by your house," Jennifer says, ready to hurdle any obstacle in her way.

Jake walks over to her, takes his coat and her car keys from her, but rather than slipping into his coat like she expected, he throws it over one of the stools at her kitchen island.

"May I?" he asks, requesting her coat with his open hand.

Jennifer reluctantly hands it to him, feeling like he's going to turn her down -- take her coat away and tell her that they should just lay low for the day.

But as soon as he has her grey peacoat in his hands, he spins her around and slips her arms through the sleeves. Then, he places his mouth right next to her ear and say, "Of course I'm driving."

Chapter Nine

A Picture is Worth a Thousand Words

Jake parks the car on the street at the base of Fred's driveway. Even though he hasn't been banished from this particular crime scene, he doesn't want to literally leave their tracks in the driveway, and as he told Jennifer, "It's supposed to snow again at 9:00 AM. That snow can cover our footprints, but I wouldn't count on it covering tire tracks."

Jennifer tucks her cold hands in her pockets and squints her eyes against the sun that is reflecting off the newly fallen snow. Looking up, she sees some dark clouds on their way, so she basks in the sun's warmth, which will be disappearing soon.

"This neighborhood feels like a movie set," Jake says, shutting his door and tucking his keys in his pocket.

Jennifer turns her attention to the houses surrounding Fred's and knows exactly what Jake means. Each house in this sleepy neighborhood looks like a storybook home. They have grey shingles on their peaked roofs, and most of the houses have small gingerbread-like windows with vines that cover and cling to the exterior brick or stone.

All of the houses in her view have a wreath hanging on their front door. One wreath is made of large green, gold, silver, and red jingle bells, while the others burst with vibrant green garland and dark brown pine cones that Jennifer imagines smell like cloves. The house across the street from Fred's has a wooden Santa sign wishing those who pass "Holiday Blessings" and the house right next to Fred's has a vintage sleigh dotted with three small pine trees on its front porch.

All of the cars parked in driveways look like marshmallow igloos, seeing as how the morning snowfall hasn't been dusted off of them yet.

She wishes they could talk with the neighbors, but she imagines the majority of them are just waking up. They're probably in flannel pajama pants and soft sweatshirts. She pictures them snuggling into their cozy socks before heading down to the kitchen to brew their morning coffee or tea as they look out at the glittering snow.

Jennifer loves when the streets are quiet like this. It's why she loves big snowfalls. Everything gets covered in a glimmering sheen of silence. When she was little she would say, "Sound is still there, but it's frozen. Don't worry, it'll be back in the spring when the ice thaws. That's when things get noisy."

Her dad would always laugh and take her by the hand when she said this.

Jake's phone goes off, pulling her out of that memory. Jake quickly looks at it, shakes his head, and shoves his phone back in his pocket.

"What is it?"

"Walk in my same steps, just to be on the safe side," Jake says, ignoring Jennifer's question and turning to move up Fred's driveway.

"Jake," Jennifer says, planting her small bootprint inside of Jake's giant print. "What did the text say?"

"It was my dad. He said Matt Kealy claims that those plates were stolen from him. He had this whole story about vanity plates, the holidays, and some other garbage."

"Oh," Jennifer says, seeing Jake's body tense. "Did your dad believe him? Did his story check out?"

Jake shrugs. "I guess so," but there's no "guessing" when it comes to Police Chief Jefferson Hollow. Jefferson doesn't make definitives until he's certain, so if he believes Matt's story then they should as well. What's strange to Jennifer is that Jake's acting like he wanted Matt to be guilty of trying to run them off the road.

Jennifer takes another step inside Jake's step, and hating the silence barrier that just developed, she says, "You know, I think your feet are bigger than the abominable snowman--" but before she can say another word, she runs directly into Jake's back.

"What is it?" Jennifer asks, seeing Jake frozen in his own steps.

"Look," he says, and she follows his finger.

Trailing up to Fred's house is a fresh set of tracks. They're not quite as big as Jake's but they're larger than Jennifer's, and they're deep and messy-- as if these footprints were eager, focused, and in a hurry.

"They're only going *to* the house," Jennifer says, and Jake unlatches his gun holster when they both come to the same realization: Whomever went into Fred's house this morning never came out. They're still in there.

"Go wait in the car," Jake says.

"That's not happening," Jennifer says. "You can't call for backup since you're possibly not supposed to be here, so I'm all you got."

Jake doesn't feel like he has time to argue with her, and he knows Jennifer. When she says she's not going to do something, she's not going to do it.

"Stay behind me, then, you hear me?"

Jennifer nods. Jake's eyes are round with worry, and she never disagrees with him when his eyes are like that.

They silently make their way to Fred's front door. It's unlocked. Unlatched. And only open a crack.

Jake grabs hold of Jennifer's hand, and they both duck under the caution tape and step into the stone entryway.

The house is even darker than Jennifer remembers, or maybe that has to do with her eyes going from the glaring sun outside to this lightless entryway. She feels a stone beneath her wobble left and right, and since she wouldn't be able to see a hand waving in front of her face, she decides the best thing to do is take Jake's arm. Linked together, they both blindly feel their way through the entry hall.

Before they curve around to the kitchen, Jennifer can smell the smoke. Then she hears a sound that shreds her heart -- someone is ripping paper. *The books,* she thinks, quickly followed by the conclusion: *someone is burning the books.* She knows that Fred has an old fire stove in his family room, she remembers seeing it yesterday.

When they turn the corner, the family room is full of smoke that's creeping into the kitchen like an eerie evening fog, but it doesn't cover the fact that someone has ransacked the house. Or, more specifically, the kitchen cabinets. In fact, every pudding box is torn open and left strewn across the kitchen floor.

But Jennifer isn't concerned with those pudding boxes. She's concerned with the fire that she knows is consuming Fred's books.

Jake pulls a handkerchief from his back pocket and whispers, "Put this over your nose and mouth and stay low."

Jennifer covers the bottom of her face as she and Jake once again blindly move through Fred's house, but this time, they're blinded by the stinging vapors of smoke. Jennifer's shaky foot finds the second step down into the family room, and that's when she sees something move. Jake sees it too; his eyes become focused like a predator. The form is to the left of the fire stove, and it's against the back wall where Jennifer knows the Dickens books are.

Once again her mind locks in on a single conclusion: Whomever is in here is burning the evidence she is now certain leads to answers.

"Freeze," Jake yells, but the body does the opposite. With the agility of a gazelle, the form jumps behind the couch and out of sight, and before they know it, the intruder is in a full sprint and dashes straight past them.

"Stay here," Jake yells at Jennifer, and before she can argue, Jake has taken off after the body, which Jennifer can now see is a man.

She can't make out much else except that he's wearing baggy sweats, has a black stocking cap on, and has a handkerchief tied around the lower half of his face. She also sees that Jake is right on his trail.

The smoke from the fire stove keeps billowing out into the room. Jennifer, now very thankful for the handkerchief, moves closer to the stove and sees that its door is fully ajar. Smoke pours out of that door, but that's not Jennifer's main concern. Just as she feared, the Dickens books are wrapped inside the hungry flames of the fire.

"No," Jennifer yells through her handkerchief. She quickly reaches out for the fire poker she remembers seeing next to the stove yesterday. Clumsy in her movements, she haphazardly knocks over the entire set of brass fireplace tools which *clang* and *clink* against each other and the stone ground. Bending down, she feels for the poker.

When she finds it, she grips the handle tightly, anchors the pointed end around one of the inflamed books and pulls. The book falls to the floor and embers spring out of it like a mini firework show. Jennifer grabs a nearby blanket and smothers the small flame that is ready to consume the book.

With at least one book partially saved, she drops the poker to the floor, investigates the dark, tube-shaped chimney of the stove, and finds the damper. It's completely closed, which is why the fire smog is unrelenting. She fully opens the damper, but getting the smoke to filter through that opening is like trying to empty a bathtub through a straw.

Jennifer's eyes burn and she coughs when she feels the smoke infiltrating her lungs.

She needs clean air.

She heads to the windows that she knows are in Fred's bedroom and throws them open. Sticking her head out of them, she gulps in the crisp, cold winter air. She stays there for a minute and sees that some of the smoke from the family room is also finding its escape through the windows.

Covering her mouth, she walks back into the main part of the house. The smoke is still heavy, so Jennifer moves toward the front door. She needs to air out this house as soon as possible so she can open that book and finally get to the bottom of this Fred Gailey murder.

When she makes the turn to the entryway, she's once again greeted with complete darkness. She only takes a few steps before a stone loosens beneath her and sends her completely off her balance. Her ankle rolls, and she falls onto the rock ground.

"Ow," she says, as she reaches down and cradles her leg that caught all of her weight. She feels around her calf for any injuries. Her tights are ripped and her deep maroon dress is crumpled around her, but she doesn't feel any cuts or scrapes. There's just the promise of a very unattractive bruise that her mother is definitely going to comment on.

She anchors her hands against the ground, and her eyes softly adjust to the darkness. The rock that took her down is right next to her -- having loosened itself from its spot. She crawls with the rock in her hand to anchor it back in place, but there's something where the rock should be. Something thin. Something malleable but with a bit of stiffness to it.

Jennifer pulls it from its hiding spot, and even though she can't see it, she knows the feel of it.

It's a photograph.

Remaining on her hands and knees, Jennifer crawls across the floor, jiggling every rock she gets her hands on. When another one rattles under her grip, she pries it up. There's another photo.

And with every rock she removes, there's another photo she collects. Until finally she is at the front door with five photos in her hands.

She stands up and is about to open the front door when Jake flings it open.

"I lost him," Jake says, out of breath. "But I got a good look at him. It was a young guy. Maybe eighteen or twenty. Blonde hair. And he was so fast." Jake bends over and puts his hands on his knees.

"Look at these," Jennifer says. "I found these under the rocks in the entryway."

Jake stands up and moves next to Jennifer. The first picture is of Fred Gailey, maybe taken a few years ago. He's standing outside a large red building, and he looks so happy and proud.

"Where is that?" Jennifer asks.

"Not sure," Jake says. "Wait a minute," he says, when Jennifer flips to the next picture. He grabs it from her hands. "That's the kid I just chased," he says, looking at the young boy who Fred Gailey is proudly standing next to. "He's a few years younger, but that's definitely him," Jake says incredulously. Fred and the young man are photographed in front of the same building from the first picture. Jake is absolutely stunned by this, but then he looks over at Jennifer. She's as white as the snow that is starting to come down again.

"What is it?" Jake asks.

Jennifer doesn't say anything. Instead, she holds up the next picture. It's Fred and he's smiling warmly. But the important part is that he has his arm affectionately around the man from 9N. The same man they found dead this morning.

Chapter Ten

Pelznickel is a Real Thing?

Back in her apartment, Jennifer places the Dickens novel she saved from the fire and the photographs from Fred's house on her countertop.

"You check on 9N," Jennifer tells Jake, who moves to the back of her place and grabs the binoculars. "We have to make sure they take those books with them."

Jake nods.

Knowing that Captain Sharb isn't going to listen to anything Jake has to say, let alone take a request from him, Jake texts his dad and asks him to grab the books from the victim's closet.

As Jake points the binoculars toward 9N, Jennifer grabs the dish soap from the kitchen and runs around the corner to her bathroom. Throwing open the doors under her sink, she pulls out her bag of cotton balls, heads back to the kitchen, and mixes up a soapy bowl of water.

Then, she carefully opens the cover of the Dickens novel. The pages of the book are covered in black soot, and the front cover -- the part Jennifer is the most interested in -- is charred like the inside of a well-used chimney.

Yet, the title page is only slightly smudged with fire remnants, so Jennifer easily reads the title, *A Tale of Two Cities*, as she dips a cotton ball into the soapy solution.

"The officers are clearing out 9N's closet," Jake says. "And my dad just text back and said he'll get the books."

"Good," Jennifer says, completely focused on her cotton ball procedure. Jake joins her at the kitchen counter. He watches as she carefully runs the solution-dipped cotton ball over the soot-coated novel. The cotton ball turns completely black. Jennifer continues to move the doused cotton balls slowly and carefully across the page until finally, they see the full message and the sticker below the soot.

"*33314 To keep the Christmas Spirit Alive.*" Jennifer says, reading the inscription. "What in the world does that mean?"

"On it," Jake says, pulling a pad of paper and pencil from Jennifer's junk drawer. This is what Jake does. He can basically crack any code or puzzle in a fraction of the time it takes an average person, as long as he has silence and concentration.

Jennifer doesn't give him either of those when she fully reveals the sticker in the book. "Jake, look at this," she says, angling the book toward him. The sticker on the inside cover is peeled and faded, but the word, which is scrolled across the label in black ink, clearly spells out:

Pelznickel

"Pelznickel," Jake repeats, but his pronunciation of the word is as slow as a lost snail.

"What in the world does that mean?" Jennifer asks. " Do you think it's a place? A person? A sticker that someone just slapped in this book without much thought?" The questions fall out of her as her eyes re-examine the word.

Jake looks at her, at the book label, and then at the number combination he's supposed to decipher.

"Which one do you want me to work on?" Jake asks. "The label or the number inscription?"

Jennifer sometimes forgets that Jake can really only focus on one thing at a time. While she has at least three stories, a constant scrolling of her to-do list, and ideas about crafts, projects, and lesson plans spinning through her head every minute she's awake, Jake's mental focus is much more defined.

"You do the numbers," Jennifer says, with a nod. "I'll research this 'Pelznickel.'"

Grabbing her laptop, she heads to her couch and plops down on the soft, white cushions. She plugs the word "Pelznickel" into her computer's search engine, and the first thing to pop up is some kind of creature. It has giant, curved horns coming out of its head; its face is pale and skeletal with a large black smile taking up the entire lower half; and the creature is covered in fur. Dingy fur. Jennifer can barely look at the photograph of the fur without wanting to vacuum it.

She leans closer to her computer screen and what she reads makes her heart and her mouth gasp.

"It's Santa Claus," she says. She continues to read.

There are various names for Santa Claus. Some are common and known to many,

such as Kris Kringle or St. Nicholas. But there are others that are a bit less familiar. For

instance, Pelznickel.

"Unbelievable," Jennifer says as she continues to read how the name "Pelznickel" was a name created by Germans and preserved by the Pennsylvanian Dutch.

Pelznickel, or Belznickel, is often depicted wearing a mask with a long tongue, and he

wears dirty, tattered clothes. He carries a switch in his hand to beat the naughty children

and carries cakes and nuts in his other hand for the good children.

"Well, that's creepy," Jennifer says, as she reads more about Pelznickel and his desire to "reform" naughty children with the powers in his switch.

"I got it," Jake says, throwing down his pencil and proudly looking up from the pad of paper. "But you're not going to like it."

"It can't be worse than this guy," Jennifer says, returning to the kitchen and turning her computer toward him.

Jake retracts his head and grimaces when he sees the dead-eye mask and long tongue. "What is that?"

"That, my friend, is Pelznickel. Also known as..." Jennifer pauses, "Santa Claus."

"That is *not* the Santa Claus I know." Jake says, shivering at the sight of the ghoulish smile and dead eyes on the horned creature. "And what kind of fur is that?" he asks, getting closer to the screen. "Is it rodent fur?"

"Okay, I can't even think about that," Jennifer says, quivering at the mere idea of rodents. She isn't afraid of spiders; she has no problems with bats, but something about small nails connected to tiny legs attached to a fur-coated body that scurries low to the ground just does her in. "Tell me about this code."

"You ready for this? The numbers come out to 9N," Jake says, and Jennifer feels chills fall down her spine. "The 333 is the 9, obviously, and then 14 corresponds with the letter N if you count the letters of the alphabet."

"So this set of books that was in Fred's house would have led someone to 9N -- the apartment where we found a man murdered this morning and the apartment someone launched pudding-filled balloons from?"

"Well, this specific book leads them there," Jake says. "We can't be sure if the same message is in the other books."

"Which are now a pile of ashes," Jennifer says, despondently.

"And," Jake says, his face changing from informative to skeptical, "I'm not convinced someone would know that the 9N referenced in this code led to the apartment across the way. There are, what, three large apartment buildings around town?"

"Two," Jennifer says. "And this is the only one with nine stories." Jennifer remembers this fact from her apartment search three years ago.

Jake runs his hands through his hair and paces around her kitchen. "So Fred knew the guy in 9N; we know that from the pictures, but why would he reference 9N's apartment in a code?"

"And the guy in 9N was a Santa somewhere, and the book label literally means Santa," Jennifer says, wishing these pieces of information would lock together rather than float separately in her mind. There's also the younger guy they found in Fred's house today, who was there to destroy the Dickens books. He must know more about these books, hence the in-house bonfire, but how does he fit in with Fred and the victim in 9N?

Before Jennifer can let her mind dig into any more details, her phone goes off. She looks at her phone and sees a message from Matt Kealy.

Matt: Hey, it looks like I'm going to have to go out of town sooner than I thought, so I
know it's last minute, but how about we grab that drink tonight?

"Who is it?" Jake asks, seeing Jennifer's face turn from intrigued to terrified.

Jennifer thinks about hiding the message. She even thinks about lying and just saying it's her mom, but she can't do that to Jake.

"It's Matt Kealy from work," Jennifer says. "He wants to have that drink tonight."

"You mean the guy who almost killed us in the car chase?"

Jennifer's shoulders fall and she looks at Jake. "Come on. Your dad said he reported the plates as stolen--"

But Jennifer's words stop there. *The plates.* The letters on the plates. She looks back at the sticker in the book: *Pelznickel.*

"Uh, Jake," Jennifer says, turning the book toward him. "Do you remember the letters on those plates Kealy reported stolen."

They both look at each other as the letters from the plates run through their heads:

In that moment, Jennifer makes two definitive conclusions.

One: somehow Matt Kealy's license plates, the car that tried to kill them yesterday, the sticker in this book, and the murders are all connected.

Two: There's no way she's not going on this date tonight with Matt Kealy, no matter what Jake argues. Because she can feel in her bones that Matt will lead to some answers, and that's the route she wants to take.

Chapter Eleven

Judy's Diner Serves up Information

Not even when she lived with her very restrictive mother did Jennifer have this many rules for going out. She and Jake are at Judy's, their usual spot. It's a diner that's been in town for over sixty years.

It's not a big place by any means, but it's big enough to be the most popular breakfast spot in Middlebridge. It has a curved counter that lines the entire right side, and that's where the morning regulars sit, drink coffee, order their eggs, and read the newspapers and magazines that are replaced and replenished every morning by Doug Caster.

Doug, who eats at Judy's every morning, is known around town for two things. The first is that he's the town's main exterminator. As the slogan on his van says, "Don't be bugged, call Doug." And the second thing he's known for is that for at least twenty years, Doug has gone around town every morning to gather and buy the day's papers and publications. That way he can bring them to Judy's for everyone to enjoy.

Jake and Jennifer give a wave to Doug and the others sitting at the counter, which has garland covered in white lights and red bows swagged all around it. There are three small Christmas trees dotting the counter, and Jennifer can see that Doug is enchanted by these trees and their twinkling lights while Jim Shriner looks beyond annoyed that they're blocking his view of everyone. Jim is a house painter, but what he really loves is drawing. Jennifer once had him come into her second-grade class to give a drawing lesson, and she's never seen Jim so alive and happy.

"Hi, my favorites," Judy, the owner who also works the register, waits on customers, and always has a pot of coffee in her hands, yells at Jake and Jennifer. "Your table is open."

This is what Jennifer loves about Middlebridge. Even though some parts of it are still a mystery and unexplored by her, like Fred's neighborhood, there are also these corner pockets, like Judy's, that truly are like home. Jennifer loves that she has a table here, that she's known the owner her whole life, and that as she and Jake make their way to the corner of the diner, Jennifer smiles and says hello to every person that they pass.

Their table is actually a booth on the far side of the diner. It's nestled in the corner, which means it's the perfect place to hide while also being the perfect vantage point to see everyone in the place.

Their booth is also dripping in garland, and there's a small plug-in Christmas tree at the edge of the table. Jennifer has barely sat down and taken off her coat by the time Jake slides a piece of paper to her. On it, it says:

The Rules for Tonight

Rule 1: No eating or drinking with Matt Kealy (easiest way to slip you something)

Rule 2: You must stay in a public place the entire time

Rule 3: I will watch you the entire date (non-negotiable)

Rule 4: Matt Kealy is never allowed to touch you

Rule 5: No ponytails, necklaces, or dangling earrings (they're an assaulter's dream)

Rule 6: You take pepper spray on your keychain

Rule 7: If you ever, EVER, feel like you are in danger, wave your hand in the air. I will step in.

"I won't agree to this meet-up unless you agree to these rules," Jake says, seriously.

Jennifer notices how Jake refuses to call her meeting with Matt a date. Although, she's not sure she wants to call it a date either. Eyeing the list, Jennifer thinks these are rather reasonable restrictions, but before she can say so, Judy -- wide-hipped, strong-voiced, brown-haired Judy -- comes over to their table.

"How are my two favorites?" Judy asks, and without a moment's hesitation, she flips Jake's cup over, fills it with coffee and hands him two creams. "Jennifer, how's your mom?"

Everyone in town knows Jennifer's mom, Eleanor, seeing that her mom lived here for fourteen years and Eleanor is always one to leave an impression.

"She's good. Getting ready for the holidays. I'm talking to her tonight and then flying out to see her and the family on Christmas Eve in two days."

"You give her my love," Judy says, winking at Jennifer. Then, Jennifer feels herself unintentionally wait for the question she always waits for but never gets. People in Middlebridge constantly ask about her mom, but no one ever asks about her dad.

Judy turns straight toward Jennifer and says, "You having the usual, sugar?"

And just like that, the moment's opportunity passes, and there's no way Jennifer is going to bring up her dad unless someone else does.

Quickly eyeing the menu that she knows by heart, Jennifer remembers the croissants and jam she was hoping to have with Jake this morning. That morning breakfast was hijacked by an attack on her apartment, a dead body, an in-house fire, and new clues to the murders. Feeling that she deserves a treat, Jennifer ups her order and says, "Actually, I'll have the blueberry pancakes this morning."

"That's my girl," Judy says, taking out her pad of paper and writing it down. "You want whipped cream?"

"Why not," Jennifer says. "And I'll have my usual peppermint tea."

"How about for you, Jake?"

"I'll take my usual."

"Two eggs and a side of toast coming up," Judy says. When she walks away, Jennifer sees Bradley Pritchard in the corner booth directly caddy corner from them. It's the only other booth in the place that has the same vantage point as her and Jake's booth. And Bradley Pritchard will wait hours for that spot; it's the only place he ever sits.

Bradley, who always keeps his coat and his scarf on wherever he goes also has his black fedora hat on this morning -- the one with the small red feather in it. Bradley grew up in the late 1950s, and it's like he loved that time so much that he refused to ever let go of it.

He has a newspaper in front of him, but Jennifer knows he's not reading that paper. He's eyeing everyone in the place, trying to size them up and find out any new gossip.

"About this list," Jake says, needing Jennifer's full understanding and agreement to the rules, but Jennifer is on another track.

"We'll get to the rules. I promise," Jennifer says, "but Bradley Pritchard is here."

Jake leans back in the booth, and without even hesitating, he looks straight at Jennifer and says, "Then go do your digging, girl. Oh, and..." Jake says, grinning like a secret-filled child, "don't forget to smile. You know how he loves your smile."

"Oh, shut up," Jennifer playfully says, and she gives Jake a small shove as she gets up from the booth. Not that Jake is wrong. Bradley Pritchard does love her smile. And her personality. And her looks. And everything about her. That's why he's happy to impress her with any and all information he has on the people that live in this town. For everyone else, he's tight-lipped and straight-eyed, but with Jennifer, it's like all of him turns into uncooked dough.

Jennifer says hi and smiles at the ladies who go to her church, the couple who runs the pharmacy downtown, and Erin Tee, who makes the most beautiful candles in town.

And then she gets to Bradley Pritchard's table.

"Well, Jennifer Hunter," Bradley says, folding his paper and tossing it to the side like it is a piece of coal compared to the shiny diamond that just appeared.

"Hello, Bradley," Jennifer says, and she gives him a grin that makes his eyes light up with hope and possibility. Jennifer knows her smiles and sweet words are harmless. Bradley is eighty-two years old. He's also been married four times, his last wife having died two years ago.

"I never expect to see an angel, and then you appear," Bradley sweetly says, reaching out and grabbing Jennifer by the hand. "But I guess that's the way angels work." He gestures to the open spot across from him, gives her his full attention and says, "I'm guessing you're here to talk about the fella who was murdered."

This is what Jennifer loves about Bradley. He's a straight-shooter. No small talk, just right to the point.

"I am," Jennifer says.

"But the question is, which one do you want to know about?" Bradley asks, and Jennifer almost falls out of the seat she's just taken. Somehow, Bradley knows about *both* murders. She doesn't even understand how that's possible seeing that the murder of the man in 9N was just discovered a few hours ago. "Oh, yes," Bradley says when he sees her surprise. "I know all about Fred *and* Earl." He takes a proud swig of his coffee and confidently leans back.

The man in 9N must be named Earl, Jennifer thinks, and she stores this in her memory so she can tell Jake all these details when she returns to their table.

"You see, Fred and Earl were Santas together way back in the day."

"What?" Jennifer says, cursing herself for not having brought her purse with her; then she could take out her pen and notepad and write this down.

"Oh, yes," Bradley says, "About thirty years ago -- before your sweet face was born," he says, winking at Jennifer. "Fred and Earl were the talk of the town when it came to playing Santa. In fact, it was right around when you were born that they took their Santa Clausing to Chicago. Went to some fancy department store downtown, and they never did dress the part back in Middlebridge again. A shame if you ask me," Bradley says.

"Did you know Fred and Earl?" Jennifer asks, trying to suss out where Bradley might be getting his information -- from himself or a different source.

"I knew them a while back, but I haven't spoken to either of them for over ten years. That's when they had their falling out."

"What do you mean?"

"I never got all the details, but something with Fred's brother. He wanted a building of theirs, and Earl refused. Drove a wedge between Fred's brother and Earl, which drove a wedge between Fred and Earl."

"Really?" Jennifer says, completely enthralled.

"But the way I hear it," Bradley says, leaning in, "Fred and Earl made up. And Fred's brother got kicked to the friendship curb.

That's what I hear; although, you know I'm not one to listen to gossip."

As Bradley pours information out of him, Jennifer tells herself to commit this all to memory: *Fred and Earl were Santas together. Fred has a brother. The brother caused issues between Fred and Earl.*

"Do you know Fred's brother's name by any chance?"

Bradley scratches his nose that has broken blood vessels at the tip of it. The skin on his face hangs loose like an unused sail, and his lips are peeling and cracked. "You know, I can't recall his name. He never lived here, and I don't take much bother with people that don't take much bother with our town."

"I can understand that," Jennifer says, smiling at his earnest responses.

"There's that smile I love," Bradley says. "Now, when are you going to dump that old dud Jake and come be my girlfriend?"

"Come on, Bradley," Jennifer says. "You know Jake and I are just friends. And if I were going to have eyes for anyone, it would be you."

"Not what I hear," Bradley says, and then he impishly takes a swig of his coffee.

"What exactly have you heard?" Jennifer asks.

"Oh, you know," Bradley says, "Just that you've got a possible date with that new guy in town. The teacher. Matt Kealy."

"How in the world do you know about that?" Jennifer asks, completely floored by the powers of knowledge that Bradley possesses. "And Matt Kealy has been here for two years," Jennifer says. "I don't think we can still call him 'new' anymore."

"I can call him whatever I want since he's trying to steal the girl I love," Bradley says. "And the way I see it, he doesn't talk to anyone in town, he's not on any teams or committees, and he's never at town events, so that makes him as new as a stranger that came to town today."

"Who are you gossiping about now?" Judy says, coming over to Bradley's table and putting down a bowl of steaming oatmeal and a side of nuts and fresh berries.

Bradley slides his meal in front of him, and Jennifer half expects him to ignore Judy's question. She knows Bradley has been coming in here for decades, but that doesn't mean he feels indebted to socialize with anyone he doesn't see fit to socialize with.

"Just commenting on our favorite girl Jennifer here possibly going on a date with that non-town-participant Matt Kealy," Bradley says.

"You're going out with Matt Kealy? The teacher?" Judy asks, but it's not surprise or even wonder in her voice when she asks this. There's something else. A worry. A strain. And it gives Jennifer pause.

"I haven't agreed to anything yet,"Jennifer says. "And it's not like it's a date or anything. We're going to simply get together and talk about school."

"Good," Judy says. "Don't trust that guy."

"Why?" Jennifer asks, getting a terrible feeling in her stomach from the look on Judy's face. "Has he done something?"

"It's a feeling I get about him," Judy says. "And my feelings are always right. Plus, he's come in here twice and both times he asked if we had oat milk for his coffee. What kind of place does he think we're running here? We serve our oats hot and steamy, not in liquid form."

"Hot and steamy is the only way to serve them," Bradley says, his full attention now on his breakfast. Judy pats Bradley on the shoulder and tells Jennifer her order will be at her table in just a minute. Seeing that Bradley's attention has gone from gossip to food, Jennifer gives him a "thanks," and let's him kiss her hand before she gets up and returns to Jake.

Within seconds she tells Jake everything that Bradley told her, and Jake writes it down, trying to connect all the dots that are floating around in his notebook and their heads.

"There's something else," Jennifer says, wanting to tell Jake about the way Judy warned her about Matt. But then she thinks better of it. If she tells Jake that Judy doesn't trust Matt, then there's no way Jake will agree to let her go out with him tonight, and Jennifer is determined to get answers from Matt tonight.

"What is it?" Jake asks, when he sees her eyes grow to the size of grapes. That's her tell-tale sign that she's either worried or hiding something.

"The rules," Jennifer says, grabbing the piece of paper Jake wrote the list on. "I wanted to let you know that I agree to these rules."

And that settles it. Tonight she'll be on a date with a man who is not only linked to the murders through some weird license plate situation but also the man in town that people don't seem to trust.

I really know how to pick them, Jennifer thinks as she sips her steaming peppermint tea.

Chapter Twelve

It Could Have Been a Nice Date

After Jennifer agreed to Jake's rules for her meet-up with Matt, she needed to do some maneuvering, seeing as Matt's suggestion for a drink broke Jake's rule #1.

So, she text Matt, apologizing and saying that she couldn't actually go get a drink, but was there any chance he'd be interested in building a gingerbread house with her instead. She saw the three dots on her phone alert her to the fact that he was typing, erasing, retyping, and then again erasing his response. She imagines that "gingerbread house building" was not exactly the adult hangout he was hoping for. But, eventually, he wrote back, "That could be fun. Let's do it."

And here they are.

They walk through the door of the quaint house where the smell of gingerbread immediately hits them. When they get inside, the house is more like a cabin with its creaky wooden floors and shiplap walls that are painted a distressed white. The walls are covered with wreaths, garland, and dozens of lanterns filled with burning red candles.

There are three old wooden baker's racks lined against the side wall, and they're covered with handmade stockings, knitted mittens and hats, fluffy pillows that have reindeers and santas embroidered on them, and other Christmas decorations for sale.

Traditional carols play over the speakers, and when Matt and Jennifer walk up to the hostess desk, they see that the back room not only glows in golden Christmas lights, but there are also long wooden tables covered in gingerbread house materials, including bowls overflowing with candy that will soon turn into decorative house materials. And behind the tables, lining the entire back wall, are at least seven Christmas trees -- all decorated by specific color combinations.

One tree, from its ornaments to the tinsel, is only outfitted in silver and gold. Another is navy and red with giant bows dotting almost every branch and a shiny red ribbon threaded through the entire tree.

"Okay, I have to admit. I was a bit skeptical when you suggested gingerbread house building, but this place is amazing,"

Matt says, leaning past the hostess desk to get a better look at the sleigh displayed behind the desk. The sleigh is outlined in low-lit, soft bulbs, and it holds two trays of steaming mugs filled with hot chocolate and topped with whipped cream. The chalkboard signs propped behind the mugs has the words "Warm Your Insides" scrolled across them, but Jennifer knows she can't indulge in those hot chocolate delights. Rule #1 and all.

"How do you know about this place?" Matt asks, eyeing the wrapped presents and flickering candles that trail behind the stationary sleigh.

It's a fair question, seeing as the outside of the house looks as plain as a piece of paper. But the owner, a woman named Michele Taylor, does that on purpose. She doesn't really open this place to the public. To be here, you have to be invited. And every holiday Michele decorates the place and throws some kind of traditional revelry. Even though Michele is young, only a few years older than Jennifer, her recently deceased husband, James, was white-haired, frail-boned, and triple her age. He was also one of the wealthiest men in town, and these small holiday gatherings is one of the ways Michele decides to spend the money he left her.

Jennifer has an open invitation because Jennifer not only taught Michele's twins, Nick and Nora, but Jennifer was the only teacher to actually help them. Before her, Nick and Nora were more like Tazmanian devils than children. Screaming. Hitting. Terrorizing any kid that got in their path. The first day of class, Nick even launched his backpack fully across Jennifer's classroom like he was in the Olympics for discus.

Yet, by the end of the first quarter -- and Jennifer's consistent tactics of giving the twins specific responsibilities, making them feel purposeful and welcome in class, and always holding them accountable for their actions -- the twins not only learned to listen and control their outbursts, but they also absolutely fell in love with Jennifer. They still come and see her before recess, and she always hugs them when she sees them in the hallways.

Their mother, Michele, is eternally grateful and told Jennifer she had a free pass to the holiday festivities anytime she wanted, which Jennifer is very grateful for in this moment.

"I know the owner," Jennifer lightly tells Matt. "Actually, she's the mom of two students I had -- Nick and Nora."

"The twins?" Matt asks, surprised.

"Yeah, do you know them?"

"They're in my fourth-grade class," he says, matching Jennifer's excited smile. "Elementary school is a small world," he says, and then he reaches out and puts his hand on Jennifer's back, "but thanks for inviting me. I think this will be fun."

All of Jennifer's nerves stand at attention when Matt touches her. It's not a nerve-standing-up situation because she finds Matt attractive. His curly hair is a bit too long for her liking; his teeth are a little too stained from what she can guess is from years of drinking way too much coffee, and his soft, unkept body make her think he could never go on long walks or chase down a criminal, which are both common activities in Jennifer's life. The reason her nerves go haywire, though, is because of *rule #4*. Matt's hand is on her back, and that means she's breaking rule #4.

A loud cough comes from behind them, causing Jennifer and Matt to turn around. Their eyes fall on the same thing. Jake.

"Evening, folks," Jake says, towering over Matt, who maybe reaches to 5'7". If that wasn't enough intimidation, Jake is in his full uniform, and he actually has his billy club out and is hitting it against his hand like it's a mini baseball bat.

"Evening," Matt says, his voice a bit shaky. His hand drops from Jennifer's back as he continues to stare at Jake's presence.

Jennifer gives Jake a sweetly annoyed look, which is also a reminder that she got him on the invitation list for tonight, so she can just as easily remove him from it. But that power she holds over him dissolves like snow hitting water when they walk into the main room and Michele, the owner of this place, gets one look at Jake.

Giving Jennifer a wave, a hug, and a quick, "So happy you could be here; the twins send their love," Michele eye-trails Jake, who has moved and stationed himself at the furthest table from them.

Jennifer and Matt sit at the closest table, but Jennifer keeps her gaze on the way Michele sashays over to Jake -- in her tight-fitted cream sweater, skinny jeans, and high-heeled boots. When she stands next to his table, she flips her hair and her giggles in Jake's direction, who gives that dimple smile of his.

"Wow, they really do expect you to use icing as glue," Matt says, having opened the box of gingerbread materials. He flips over the written directions and investigates the provided drawings. That's when Jennifer reminds herself that she's not here to watch women fawn over Jake; she's here to get some answers. Plus, Michele isn't Jake's type. Jennifer is sure of it.

It's not until Matt and Jennifer have the full base and roof of their gingerbread house built that Jennifer thinks she can move into the questions she's determined to ask.

The thing is, she's having more fun with Matt than she expected. They talk about the students that both of them have had, the monthly faculty meetings that both of them find completely boring, and why they love teaching so much.

She never gets to talk to anyone about teaching -- her mother despising that she even has a profession, her brother, Michael, only interested in his finance job or sentences that begin with "The stock market is…" and his wife, Julie, always judging and one-uping Jennifer whenever she even mentions teaching. Jake listens to Jennifer's stories about school, but he was the kind of student who couldn't wait to graduate and never return, so he doesn't understand her love for the classroom, and teaching, and curriculum, and homework.

But Matt is different. He's like her. And, he's proving to be much funnier than she ever expected.

"Shouldn't we be building gingerbread garages for these houses? I bet gingerbread car thievery is rampant in these gingerbread towns," Matt says. "The resale value on our gingerbread property is plummeting without a garage."

"Oh, yeah," Jennifer says, playing along. "And you know why people are stealing those gingerbread cars? It's not for the peppermint steering wheel as one might think. It's for the gumdrop wheels. Green gumdrop wheels are all the rage in the gingerbread world."

"Uh, and in the real world. I'd give my left arm for a set of gumdrop rims," Matt says, smiling at Jennifer. "In fact, they should make gumdrop bumpers. That way no one could ever do a hit and run. They could only do a hit and stick."

Jennifer laughs at this idea, and then sees her perfect segue. "Well, I could have used a gumdrop bumper yesterday. I got hit, and the person didn't even stop," she says, hoping this will lead Matt into a confession about his license plates.

"What?" Matt says, his eyes and voice bulging. "Are you okay? I mean, you look okay. Better than okay." He shyly clears his throat. "But were you hurt?"

"No, I'm fine. I just couldn't believe that someone would run straight into the back of my car and not stop," Jennifer says, thinking about what she can and cannot disclose to Matt. She hates to lie, so even though the context around her story doesn't include all the details, the information she's giving is accurate.

"Yeah, I know what you mean. Someone actually stole my license plate the other day."

"Really?" Jennifer says, her ears perking up even though she's pretending to be fully focused on covering their gingerbread roof in wafer candies.

"Well, they weren't really *my* license plates," Matt says. "They got delivered to me. And get this, it was from a guy named Fred Gailey."

Jennifer's hand jolts at the mention of Fred's name, and she knocks the wafer shingles straight off of their gingerbread house.

"Fred Gailey?" Jennifer repeats, not believing what she's hearing.

"Yeah, like the dad in *Miracle on 34th Street.*"

"Why would Fred Gailey send you a license plate?" Her voice is too eager. She can tell by the way that Matt is side-eyeing her.

"I wish I knew. All I know is that I got a package in the mail last week with a letter that said there was some kind of advertising promotion going on, and if I put these holiday vanity plates on my car I'd get $250 a week."

"Seriously?" Jennifer asks.

"Yeah, I know," Matt says, directing his focus back to the yogurt-covered pretzel fence he's building. "I'm now convinced it was a scam, but at the time it seemed legit. Plus, an extra 250 bucks a week sounded so nice. And, I thought, what could it hurt?"

"True," Jennifer says, even though in her head she's thinking about all the people those plates might have caused to get hurt. There's Fred, who is dead; Earl in 9N, who is dead, and the fact that she and Jake also almost got killed.

"Even worse," Matt says, "the person who stole the plates did something pretty bad." There's an innocence in Matt's voice when he says this. "I don't know what, but the cops called me just yesterday asking about those plates that I registered under my name last week."

"Really?" Jennifer says, egging him on.

"I should have known it was going to cause nothing but problems. The letter that came with the plates was so weird."

"What do you mean?" Jennifer asks, icing some peppermint sticks on the gingerbread windows while trying to hide her insane desire to ask hundreds of questions.

"Well," Matt says, "This is going to make me sound nuts, but not only was the letter signed by a man named Fred Gailey, but under his name he had a title. 'The Society of Santas.' That was written under his name."

Jennifer freezes like she's been put on pause.

Matt sees her open-mouth look of astonishment and voices what he's already said to himself dozens of times. "I know. I know. I should have just thrown the license plate and the letter away, but the $250 a week just sounded so good for the holidays, you know?"

He continues to talk, but it's like Jennifer's ears shut down. The pieces of what Matt is telling her fling around in her mind. So someone wanted Matt to have those plates, but why? And why would someone then steal the plates they went to so much trouble getting to Matt? And was that someone really Fred Gailey? He wasn't dead last week, which was when Matt received the package, but why would Fred send Matt a license plate? How did he even know Matt? And, what is the world is "The Society of Santas"?

She needs to talk this through with Jake. She needs his insight so they can brainstorm together.

"You okay?" Matt asks, seeing that she isn't listening to a word he's saying.

"I have to go to the bathroom," Jennifer says. And with the grace of an elephant on a tightrope, she haphazardly stands up, throws her purse over her shoulder, and makes a direct line to the bathroom.

She doesn't make eye contact with Jake, convinced that will look too suspicious. Plus, he's still being verbally accosted by Michele, who moved into the empty seat next to Jake.

He'll notice that I'm gone, Jennifer thinks to herself. *Then Jake will come and find me.* She's sure of that.

Reaching the bathroom, she pushes the door open, and even the bathroom is fully decorated in Christmas niceties -- the mirrors have swags on the top of them, and there's a cinnamon candle burning right next to the sink, which Jennifer quickly walks by. She ducks into a stall and pulls out her phone to text Jake. But there's a message waiting from her; it's from her sister-in-law, Julie.

Julie: Talked to mom tonight. She said you haven't started on the tree skirt. I really hope you don't rush it. I'd rather not have the skirt than receive a rushed version of the design you showed me, which I love, by the way. I'm sure you'll figure it out, and please let me know if you want some time management tips. I do this with my clients all the time and am happy to help you. Love you and can't wait to see you.

There is a kiss and Christmas tree emoticon after the message, but those emoticons of affection do nothing for the anxiety now growing like a vine inside of Jennifer. She needs to work on those presents. She knows this. She frustratingly sighs as she imagines Julie's view of her life. She probably thinks Jennifer sits around watching movies and eating Christmas cookies all day; little does she know that Jennifer is out trying to solve *two* murders.

Speaking of which.

She clicks out of Julie's message and writes a text to Jake.

The second she gets the message sent, the lights go out, an ear-piercing siren goes off, and a flashing red light pulses against the far wall. The alarm echoes so forcefully through the small bathroom that Jennifer tucks her phone in her purse and covers her ears. That's when the water comes. The sprinkler system above her spurts water in every direction.

"What is happening?" Jennifer yells, but she's still the only one in the bathroom.

Within seconds, her long hair that she wore down upon Jake's request, her knitted grey sweater dress that she paired with her favorite black tights and small-heeled black ankle boots are completely drenched.

The alarm continues to blare and echo to an unnerving point. Jennifer steps out of the stall and almost slips on the water that has puddled across the bathroom floor. Even the candle has gone out thanks to the sprinkler deluge, but Jennifer eventually finds her way back to the main room.

It's empty.

Not a single person, including Jake, is in there.

They must have evacuated, she thinks.

The gingerbread houses soften, collapse, and fold into themselves as the water from above saturates the tables below. Jennifer looks around the room one last time, expecting to see Jake, who she knows would never leave her behind. Then she hears a rustle. It's coming from behind her. It's coming from the Christmas trees.

A panic tears through her chest as she sees the tree shake. Someone is in there and they're about to come out. Plunging her hand in her purse, she grips the pepper spray Jake made her bring and readies herself.

Then, she sees the figure emerge from the green branches, knocking dozens of red glass ornaments to the ground when he does.

"Matt?" Jernnifer asks, squinting through the sprinkler rain and the darkness. He runs over to her.

"I didn't want to leave you," he yells over the alarm, which seems to be even louder out here, "so I hid in the tree."

Jennifer can't hold in her smile when she sees the sprigs of pine stuck in his hair. He grabs her hand and pulls her toward the back of the room rather than the front where they came in. The water continues to fall down on them, making Jennifer's feet slide and squish in her boots.

Matt pushes through a back door that Jennifer didn't even realize was there. She figures it must be an emergency exit, and she expects to see everyone who was inside standing outside that door. But she doesn't. Matt pulls her into an almost completely vacant parking lot.

A cold wind blows and hits her like a tidal wave. The water that's coating her hair and her body starts to crystalize into ice. Instinctively, she wraps her arms around herself, her teeth chatter, and all of her muscles tense up. Matt flings her coat over her, which she realizes he must have grabbed from the table before they left.

"Come on," Matt says, also shivering due to his drenched state. He grabs her hand, and Jennifer doesn't refuse. "My car is right here," he says, walking her to one of two cars that's in this back parking lot. Jake's car is out front. She knows she should go there; she knows she should refuse Matt, but she's just so cold, so when he opens the door for her, she gratefully slips into the car that will immediately block this incessant wind.

Matt shuts her in, runs around the car, and jumps in the driver's seat. He turns on the car. "Heat," he says. "We need heat."

Those words make sense to Jennifer, and they're truly her only desire at the moment. But what Matt does next, makes no sense at all. Once he has the heat on full blast, he slyly moves his hand over to the panel on the door and hits the lock button.

Jennifer's heart lurches when she looks over and sees that Matt just locked her in his car.

Chapter Thirteen

The Hidden Waterseal

Jake is going to kill her. Well, that is, if Matt doesn't kill her first. But Jennifer convinces herself that she's being completely rational, especially since Matt explained that he "always locks the doors after being car jacked in Chicago last year." His explanation paired with the police-grade pepper spray that's on her keychain is why Jennifer cooly and calmly texts Jake her whereabouts. Although, his string of texts in response are anything but cool and calm.

Jake: Get out of that car right now.

Jake: Rule #2, 3, and 7!

Jake: You are breaking all of those!

Jake: And, you're being reckless.

His text when she writes back and tells him that they are already on their way to Matt's apartment is worse. It is only three words:

Jake: Jennifer Lynn Hunter.

Whenever Jake uses her full name, she knows he's moved beyond anger. He's moved into boiling-over-and-it's-going-to-take-so-many-apologies-to-make-this-right zone.

But Jennifer doesn't feel reckless; she feels directed. Matt says his place is close, has a dryer, and he has clothes that she can borrow, but Jennifer isn't really interested in any of those factors.

She's interested in the letter.

If she can get the Fred Gailey letter then she and Jake can investigate it. They might find a clue that matches with the books or the photographs. *That will make Jake forgive me,* Jennifer convinces herself.

"This is me," Matt says as he parks his car outside the small apartment building Jennifer didn't even realize was open. They shut this building down years ago, on the order of Doug, the bug guy. And as she and Matt go inside and climb the three flights of stairs to

Matt's place, Jennifer isn't fully convinced this place *should* be open. The metal stairwell is dark, filmy, and it creaks under each of their steps. When they get to the third floor and walk down the brown carpeted hallway that still has remnants of cigarette smoke in it, Jennifer swears she can see the carpet moving. Crawling. And it gives her the chills.

"Home sweet home," Matt says when they get to apartment 3C.

He proudly opens the door, and when Jennifer walks into the beige-carpeted apartment, she would describe the place as anything other than sweet.

Barren. Bland. And Dingy. Those are the words that come to her mind.

Matt has absolutely nothing on the walls, except for the buttercream paint that's chipping in the corner near her. He doesn't have a Christmas tree, a candy cane, or anything to show it's the holiday season. His carpet is dotted with random stains, and the main room is completely boxed in by walls. Jennifer scans the room, sees one door, which she assumes goes to the bedroom, but that leaves her at a complete loss in regard to where the kitchen is. Does he even have a kitchen?

"Let me grab you some dry clothes," Matt says, heading to the door off the main room. Jennifer takes the opportunity while he's away to scour the place for the letter.

Matt has books and papers spewed all across his coffee table, which is blocky and looks like the legs were gnawed on by a dog. Jennifer quickly shuffles through the papers, keeping an eye on the bedroom door. She doesn't find anything but old graded papers, magazines, and piles of receipts on the table, so she quickly dashes to the back of the main room to see what's there.

She finds a door that is hidden behind the pop-out wall in the center of the room where Matt has hung his giant television. She wants to see what's on the other side of that door, but she's too afraid Matt will come back and find her snooping about. She needs more time.

Running back to where she was standing when Matt left, she tries to think of an excuse that will allow her to be alone in his place.

"Here we go," Matt says, coming out of the bedroom door. "Flannel pants and a henley."

"Oh, no," Jennifer says, eyeing the fabric that will have her roasting like the proverbial chestnut over an open fire. "No, no no," she repeats.

"What? Do you not like the color?"

"You think I care about the color?" Jennifer asks. "I'll sweat to death if I wear those. Do you have a t-shirt and maybe some lighter-fabriced pants or even shorts?"

"I'll see what I can do," Matt says, turning back into the bedroom.

Jennifer takes the opportunity when Matt is gone to run through the door she discovered. It leads to Matt's kitchen, and she almost faints when she steps into it.

There are dirty pans piled up on the stove, including one with crusted egg remnants in it, which she can only hope is from his breakfast this morning. There are crumbs all over the counter top, and he has dozens of old pizza boxes piled up next to his garbage can.

She can't believe he lives like this; his classroom is never *this* messy. Plus, Jennifer can't help but think about Jake's house. It's this adorable cottage that's been in his family for over a century. More importantly, she would eat off Jake's bathroom floor with how clean and meticulous he is; she's not even sure she'd eat off a plate in Matt's house.

Then she sees a collection of envelopes and papers on the small table at the end of the kitchen. She quickly runs over to them and scans each one.

There it is, she exclaims in her mind when she gets to the third letter. She eyes the bottom of the letter and sees:

Fred Gailey

The Society of Santas

Shoving the letter in her inner coat pocket, Jennifer scatters the pile of papers and runs into the family room. She doesn't make it back to her original spot in time, but she pretends to be interested in the beer bottle lamp Matt has on his side table in the corner closest to the kitchen.

Her heart pounds like a shoe in a dryer as she makes up some weird compliment about the lamp, which leaves Matt beaming.

"Do you want to change in the bathroom?" Matt asks, but after seeing the state of his kitchen, Jennifer isn't going anywhere near Matt's bathroom.

"Can I just change in your bedroom?" Jennifer asks.

"Sure. Be my guest. I'll change after you," Matt says, handing her a t-shirt and cotton pants; he keeps the flannel pants and sweatshirt for himself.

When Jennifer walks into his bedroom, she doesn't even bother looking around. She immediately drops the clothes to the floor and takes out Fred's letter. She examines every inch of it.

The font is unlike any she's ever seen. It's thick and almost looks wet, like those old-timey letters and books people would write using a quill and a bottle of ink. The paper is thick, heavy, and almost has a yellow tinge to it.

Diving straight into the message, Jennifer reads every line. Just as Matt said, there's a whole song and dance about a promotional opportunity promising $250 a week for using these particular plates, but then Jennifer sees something at the top corner of the letter. It's faded. Hidden.

She holds the letter closer to her face. It's a watermark, but it's too dark to make out its details. Moving over to Matt's dresser, she holds the letter up to the silver lamp he has. She feels her blood freeze when she sees that the watermark clearly spells out the word "Pelznickel." Not only that. It's in the same script as the sticker inside the Dickens book.

"I knew it," Jennifer says, utterly pleased with herself. She thinks about texting Jake right then and there, but when she looks up at Matt's dresser every thought falls out of her head. There's a shelf above the dresser, and it's full of books. More specifically, it's filled with one book.

Jennifer silently reads title after title, and they're all the same. *A Christmas Carol; A Christmas Carol; A Christmas Carol; A Christmas Carol.*

The chill that runs through her puts her earlier frozen state to shame. "Oh my God," Jennifer says so loudly that she puts her hand over her mouth to stop from screaming.

Most of the copies Matt has of the book are regular copies found at any book store, but there's one version of *A Christmas Carol* on his shelf that sticks out from all the others. It's the version that's wrapped in brown leather. The title is written in gold script, and it has gold-edged pages. The leather is a different color, but this book matches the set at Fred's and the set in Earl's apartment. Jennifer reaches up to grab the book, but then she hears Matt's voice.

"Everything okay?" Matt asks. He must have heard her almost yell just seconds ago.

She whips her head around, and her eyes fall to the small crack at the bottom of his bedroom door. It's letting in the light from the main room, but there are two dark spots. They're the exact size of Matt's feet.

He's standing outside the door.

"Jennifer, you okay?" he asks, but she can barely believe this is happening, let alone respond to that question. "You're making me nervous."

I'm making him nervous? she sarcastically thinks. She's not the one who has dozens of copies of a book that has inspired a killing spree in the last 48 hours. She's also not the one who has an edition of *A Christmas Carol* that matches the missing book from both crime scenes.

Jennifer definitively decides: she needs that book.

With a shaking hand, she reaches up to grab it, but when she pulls it out, the other books that were leaning on it slant and tilt, causing two books to fall off the shelf. They hit the lamp and knock down the glass bottles of cologne on Matt's dresser.

Hearing the scuffle and still not hearing a word from Jennifer, Matt decides enough is enough.

"Jennifer, I'm coming in," he says. And before she can stop him, he opens the door and closes it behind him.

Chapter Fourteen

A Christmas Spray of Caution

"You're not changed," Matt says, eyeing the clothes he gave Jennifer, which are tossed on the floor. He looks up at her with a confused smile, but then his face turns to marble. He looks directly at the letter and book that she's tightly clutching.

"What are you doing with those?" Matt asks. A cutting edge develops in his voice when he asks, "Did you steal that from my stuff?"

He starts to move toward her. Charge toward her.

Jennifer goes into a complete panic as the details of everything jolt through her mind:

Matt had the plates of the car that tried to kill her. Matt has this mysterious letter from

Fred Gailey, who is now dead. Matt has a collection of the exact books that are linked with the murders. Matt somehow has worked at the same school with Jennifer for two

years and only asked her out two days ago when all of this started.

Most importantly, though, Matt is now charging straight toward her with a crazed look on his face.

Before Jennifer even realizes what she's doing, she pulls the pepper spray from her purse, pops the cap, aims it directly at Matt's face, and sprays.

He melts down to the floor like the Wicked Witch of the West, clawing at his eyes while screaming in agony.

Jennifer bounds past him and runs out the door. She can still hear him screaming as she makes her way out of his apartment and down the hallway. When she hits the stairwell, she takes two steps at a time until she finally lands on the ground floor. She's convinced that she's going to have to run home. Yes, it's probably about four miles. Yes, her clothes are still damp. Yes, it's just above freezing tonight. But, she doesn't see that she has another choice.

Throwing open the apartment building door, she runs smack into Jake, who is waiting and pacing outside Matt's building.

Jake stops her mid-sprint and holds onto her by her shoulders.

"What is it? What did he do?" Jake asks, eyeing every part of Jennifer to make sure she's okay.

"He has the books," Jennifer says, frantically. "He has the book," she says, but she doesn't show Jake what she took from Matt's apartment. Instead, she tucks her arms inside his coat and lets him wrap her in a warm hug. She wishes she could hide inside Jake's skin. She'd do almost anything to escape her own skin, which feels like death and deceit are crawling across it like centipedes.

Jake doesn't understand anything Jennifer just said, but he sees the fear in her eyes and the fright that has made her pale skin even whiter. In Jake's mind, that's enough evidence to justify ripping Matt's arms off.

Still holding her tightly, Jake says, "Get in the car. Lock yourself in, and don't do anything until I get back." He's ready to storm into the building. "What's his apartment number?"

"No. Please, Jake. Just get me out of here. I want to get out of here."

"Jennifer--"

"Jake, please," her voice rips out of her as she looks up at him, and it's quickly followed by tears that run down her face.

Jake doesn't put up a fight.

He quickly escorts Jennifer to his car, looking over his shoulders as he does, and pulls away from Matt's apartment building.

They silently drive through the quiet streets, which look like they're covered in slick oil due to the melted snow that's lit up by tonight's full moon. Jennifer wipes away the tears that feel like they'll never stop while Jake eyes the book that's in her lap. It's too dark to see the title clearly, but he has a feeling it's the exact book they've been looking for. He also knows that Jennifer isn't ready to talk yet.

She keeps her eyes focused outside the window on the houses covered in the warm glow of Christmas lights. Seeing those lights and the holiday decorations remind her that there's good in the world. There are houses and apartments filled with families that laugh together, that hug and kiss, and that have warm beds they feel safe in.

She feels Jake's hand softly cover her hand, and she's so relieved that he's there with her. She can always count on him, even when she breaks his rules or makes him mad, and that fact makes her insides flood with gratefulness and love for Jake. She turns her hand over and holds his hand inside hers as well.

"You going to tell me what happened?" Jake asks.

Feeling that she can finally think and speak clearly, Jennifer says, "You're going to want to send some officers over to Matt's apartment. I pepper sprayed him, and I think I got him pretty good."

Then, she tells Jake everything -- about the letter, the watermark, the shelf of books, the copy of *A Christmas Carol* she took, and when she describes the way Matt charged toward her, her voice shakes and cracks.

"You did the right thing pepper spraying him," Jake says, knowing that Jennifer is debating this very fact. Ever since she was little Jennifer has succumb to her instincts and then questioned them right after. And for as long as Jake has known her, those instincts have always been spot-on.

He gives her hand a squeeze and then lets go of her to grab the walkie talkie from the car's dashboard. Not wanting to trigger the panic Jennifer felt back there, Jake keeps his tone calm and professional as he requests a perpetrator pick-up and gives the address. He asks Jennifer for the apartment number, which she gives. Then, Jake turns his face away because he knows that as he says, "The perpetrator has been pepper sprayed, so bring needed equipment," he can't help but smile. Just a bit.

After the confirmation that Matt and his books will be brought down to the station, Jennifer feels like she can finally breathe again. Something about Matt being on the loose -- even if he is partially blind -- and possibly knowing where she lives, made her heart quiver.

She looks down at the book in her lap, and it gives her a sense of victory. This is what they've been after. At least, she thinks this is what they've been after. Running her hands over the cover, she's just about to crack it open when Jake interrupts her.

"You want to tell me why you decided to break every rule we agreed to and then do something as stupid as to go up to that guy's apartment?" His voice is parental.

In hindsight, yes, Jennifer can see that what she did was wrong, but Jake would have done the same thing if he was in her shoes. Plus, she's not hurt, and she got exactly what they needed by doing "something as stupid as to go up to that guy's apartment." This is exactly what she bites back to him.

"You could have gotten yourself killed, do you realize that?" Jake fights back.

"But I didn't," Jennifer says.

"But you could have." Jake's voice is angry, yes, but there's more to it than that. Jennifer worried him. She didn't listen to him. In fact, she downright disobeyed him, which she knows feels completely disrespectful.

"Look, you're right," Jennifer says, waving a verbal white flag. "And I'm sorry."

"Well, I may eventually accept your apology," Jake says, and after a moment of silence he says, "Plus, I can't think this is all your fault. Someone set off the sprinkler system at Michele's place, and Matt just happened to be there to steal you away. Seems too coincidental for me."

"Yeah, what in the world happened there? One minute I'm in the bathroom and the next I'm in an indoor monsoon."

"Someone did that on purpose; I know it," Jake says. "And, there's more."

Jennifer looks over at him, and she sees him take a deep breath. "My dad called. They got the lab and autopsy results."

"And?" Jennifer asks, turning her body toward him.

"The sprig of holly was clean. But the pudding sample from Fred's and from Earl's place both had cyanide in them. That's how the men died; they were poisoned with cyanide."

"Cyanide?" Jennifer asks, completely surprised by this information.

"Yep," Jake says. "So both men were poisoned with cyanide, both men were positioned to emulate a scene from *A Christmas Carol,* both men had an oddly large amount of pudding in their house, and both men had the same set of Dickens novels. The question is: Why?"

"And," Jennifer asks with trepidation, "who's next?"

Jake eyes the book in Jennifer's lap, and she does the same. They both share the sense that this book will hold all the answers. Jennifer cracks open the cover, and looks in the upper corner. It doesn't have the hand-written message like the others. It does, however, have the Pelznickel sticker.

Jennifer flips to the title page, which has a beautiful illustration of Mr. and Mrs. Fezziwig, from *A Christmas Carol*, dancing. And then she opens to page one of the story.

"Look at this," Jennifer says, barely able to believe what she's seeing. There are number combinations next to random words and paragraphs on the first page.

"457811; 259802; 778909; and 82308," Jennifer says, reading them out loud. "What do these mean?" she asks, tilting the book toward Jake as he pulls into her parking garage.

"You have to be kidding me," Jake says, making turn after turn in her parking garage to get to the eighth floor. He glances over at the book after each turn he makes. "And some of those combinations have six numbers. The one we took from the Dickens novel you saved only had five numbers."

Jennifer quickly scan the combinations. "Actually, some of these have four numbers in the combination and some have seven," she says, frustratingly. Then she flips to the next page. There are even more combinations scattered above random words and next to random paragraphs. And, all of them have a different amount of numbers in them. Fearing the worst, Jennifer fans through all the pages in the book and sees that every single page is plagued with number combinations like they're the chicken pox.

Jake sees the exact same thing. "You can't be serious," he says.

He makes the last turn in the garage toward her parking spot, but then he slams on the brakes, sending both of them and the book flying forward.

"What in the world?" Jennifer asks, raising back up from her thrashed state, but then she sees what caused Jake's reaction. Her parking space is filled with at least three feet of gelatinous chocolate pudding.

"Seriously?" Jennifer asks. "More pudding? Who has access to all of this pudding?"

"And how did they get it to stay like that just in your parking spot?" Jake asks, eyeing the mound in wonder.

Both of them get out of Jake's car, and walk toward the pudding mountain. "How am I going to clean this up?" She looks down at her hands that are still red and cracked from cleaning the pudding off her windows in the icy cold this afternoon.

Sighing, she takes another step closer and hears a crunch under her boot. Looking down, she doesn't see anything, but something tells her not to move.

"Uh, Jake," she says, pointing to her frozen foot. "I think I stepped on something."

"Don't move," he says, throwing himself at her feet. He flattens himself against the cement and shines his flashlight under her boot. He looks up at her, and she doesn't need to hear his words. She can see in the way that Jake anxiously covers his mouth with his hand and then runs that hand through his hair that it's bad.

"What is it?" Jennifer asks.

"I need you to stay completely still," Jake says, looking around. "You've stepped on some kind of detonator."

"A detonator?" Jennifer yells so loudly that a pair of random birds flap in fear through the parking garage. They startle Jennifer so much that she jumps back. And then she realizes what she's actually done.

Her foot is off the detonator.

She looks at Jake. They stare at each other in silence, and that's when they hear it. A ticking. It's close by, but it sounds muffled.

"Run," Jake yells, grabbing Jennifer's hand.

But it's too late. The ticking turns into an alarm before the two of them can take one step.

Chapter Fifteen

Captain Sharb Gets Serious (Part II)

Suddenly, a giant *whoosh* fills the parking garage. A large piece of fabric springs out from the brown, gelatinous mound and flings pudding all over Jennifer and Jake.

"Oh, gross," Jake says, scooping pudding off his face and out of his hair. Jennifer does the same, and when she scoops a glob of pudding from right above her eye, she sees that the fabric that caused this pudding shower is actually a banner.

Whomever did this had the banner knotted to fishing line, and when Jennifer stepped on the detonator it triggered a pulley system. The banner now hangs from the ceiling above her parking spot, dripping with thick, brown pudding that falls off in loud *gloups.* That's when Jennifer sees the message on the banner. It says:

God Bless Us Every One

"That's what Tiny Tim says," Jennifer says, trying to bring Jake's attention to the banner rather than his soiled uniform, which he's attempting to wipe clean.

"What is with this person and pudding?" Jake annoyingly asks, as he clears a handful of it out from under his belt.

"Jake," Jennifer says firmly to get his attention, "the words on the banner are the final words in *A Christmas Carol."*

When Jake's eyes fall on the banner, his shoulders also fall. "This person is a total whack-job," he says. Then, remembering his duty as a Lieutenant, he says, "I'll call it in. You go get cleaned up and packed."

"Packed?" Jennifer asks.

"Yes. You're coming to my house. Your place is too dangerous for either of us. In fact, I'm walking you upstairs and then I'll come back down and call this in," Jake says, definitively.

By the time Jennifer is showered, cleaned, and packed -- having her bag mainly filled with skeins of yarn for the Christmas presents she hasn't even started -- the pudding on Jake's body and uniform has formed into a crusted shell.

Jennifer meets Jake back in the parking garage, but he's no longer alone. There are a handful of officers taping off her parking spot and Captain Sharb is standing next to Jake. Red-faced, annoyed, and tight-eyed Captain Sharb stares right at Jennifer as she walks over to them.

"Here," Jennifer says, handing Jake the towel she promised him.

Jake moves over to his police car, dumps his bottle of water on the towel, and rubs away some pudding from his face and neck.

Jennifer awkwardly stands next to Sharb, who won't stop dead-eyeing her.

"You just can't keep your nose out of police business, can you?" Sharb asks when Jennifer refuses to make eye contact with him. His accusation breaks her aloof stance.

She turns toward Sharb and looks him right in the eye. "In case you haven't noticed, this happened to me. It's not like I asked for someone to come and pudding my parking space."

"But why would this perpetrator and possible murderer feel the need to target you?" Sharb asks accusingly. "In all my years as an officer, a Lieutenant, and a Captain in the police force, there's only two reasons someone does something like this."

Jennifer feels her insides twist when Sharb keeps his eyes directly on her. He wants her to confess something, but she keeps her mouth shut.

"Either the perpetrator wants to scare someone out of following their trail or the victim has something the perpetrator wants. Now, neither of those *should* apply to you, but why do I get the feeling that they both apply to you?"

It takes all her might, but Jennifer keeps quiet.

She knows that Sharb is correct; both of those things do apply to her. She's getting closer and closer to solving these murders; she can feel it. And she also knows that in her bag -- buried deep below the yarn, her clothes, the cookie cutters, her crochet hooks, and her toiletries -- is the book from Matt's house. The book that seems to be the key to everything, even if it's filled with numbers that currently don't make any sense to her.

"I asked you a question," Sharb says, moving and standing directly in front of Jennifer. He folds his hot dog fingers in front of him and devilishly says, "Because, the way I see it, you shouldn't even be known to the murderer, and yet, here we are."

He's going to keep pushing her. She can feel it. He'll push and push until she breaks.

"Jen," Jake yells from his car. "I have to get home and shower. There is pudding literally in my ear."

Seeing her escape route, Jennifer puts a hand on Sharb's shoulder and says, "Wish I could help," and then she slips right past him. Yet, as she walks to Jake's squad car and slides into the passenger seat, she feels Sharb's judgmental and suspicious eyes remain on her.

It's not until they pull out of the parking garage and Jake starts talking that Jennifer shakes Sharb's beady-eyed look out of her mind.

"My dad called while you were in your place," Jake says, pulling out onto main street. "They picked up Kealy and got the books. Turns out he had thirteen copies of *A Christmas Carol*."

"Fourteen, technically," Jennifer says, referencing the book in her bag. "Are his eyes okay?" Jennifer asks, still worried that her pepper spraying of Matt makes her more like an impulsive skunk than a rational human.

Jake looks over at her as he turns down Fern Street. "Yes, his eyes are completely fine," he says, "but I need to tell you something." Jake's voice is as straight as a horizon line, which means that the "something" he has to tell her, is serious. Jennifer turns toward him and readies herself for the news.

"Kealy's alibi he gave for yesterday, during the car chase, Sharb says it all checks out."

Jennifer shrugs. "We knew that," she says. "We didn't have his alibi cleared, but his story checked out."

Jake awkwardly adjusts in his seat and takes a deep breath. That's when Jennifer realizes that Kealy's car-chase alibi isn't the serious news. There's more.

"Well, he also gave an alibi for the books. And it also checks out."

"What do you mean?"

Jake turns down his street, and it's the one time Jennifer has ever wanted Jake to live farther away. She doesn't want anything to interrupt what he's about to tell her.

"Kealy says the books are a gift. He says his parents give him a copy of *A Christmas Carol* every year. They send it to him a week or so before Christmas as a tradition. My dad contacted the parents, they confirmed, and they said they even have a receipt for the book they bought this year."

Jennifer looks down at her hands. *It's official,* she thinks. *I'm a monster. I pepper sprayed a completely innocent guy.*

"You couldn't have known," Jake says, knowing that her conscience is diving head first into a pool of guilt. "You did what you thought was right--"

"What book?" Jennifer asks, cutting off Jake's comforting words.

"What?"

"Which copy of *A Christmas Carol* did his parents send him this year?" Jennifer's mind becomes hyper-focused. She feels terrible about Matt, and she can't even venture into analyzing the fact that she pepper sprayed the only thing resembling a date she's had in over a year. Her only option is to make this better. She needs to solve this crime and apologize to Matt for the rest of her life.

Jake eyes Jennifer's bag, confirming what she already suspected. The brown leather copy of *A Christmas Carol* that she took and that matches the sets in Fred's and Earl's place was the newest addition to Matt's collection.

"We need a copy of that receipt," Jennifer says.

"Already on it," Jake says, pulling into his driveway. "My dad requested that Matt's parents send a photo of the receipt, and he's going to send it to me as soon as he gets it."

"Anything else?" Jennifer asks, jokingly, but then she sees that there *is* more.

Jake unbuckles his seat belt. "Officer Holtz told me some information about the books before Sharb cut her off."

"What is up with Sharb?" Jennifer asks, but Jake jumps right over that rhetorical question.

"Turns out that the Dickens novels in Earl's place, guess what was on the inside cover of all of them?"

"A Pelznickel sticker?" Jennifer asks.

"Yep. *And* the exact same number combination as the book you saved from the fire at Fred's house."

"The '33314 to keep the Spirit of Christmas alive' message?" Jennifer asks, also unbuckling her seatbelt.

"That inscription exactly. In every single Dickens book at Earl's," Jake says.

"What in the world. Well, why would the books in Earl's apartment be a code that leads to Earl's apartment-- the 9N?" Jennifer asks. "That doesn't make any sense."

"I don't think the code is to lead people to 9N anymore," Jake says, opening the car door.

"What's it for, then?" Jennifer asks, quickly hopping out of the car and catching up with him.

"That's what we're going to figure out."

Chapter Sixteen

Cracking the Christmas Carol Code

Jennifer and Jake walk up Jake's driveway as he opens his garage door. Jake never parks the squad car in his garage -- that spot is reserved for his true love. His boat. It's a gleaming white speed boat, and Jake has it hibernate in his garage during the winter. Come summer, though, he wakes up his bear of a boat and parks it in the bay. That way he can do what he loves to do everyday in the summer -- go out on the water in the early mornings and after he's finished a day at work.

Jennifer runs her hand across the boat as they make their way to his door, and as soon as she steps into Jake's house, she feels like she's at home. This old craftsman house was built by Jake's great-grandfather, and it's been passed down in his family ever since. Jake's older sister, Lindsey, who is a big-time photographer in L.A., didn't want the house, but Jake did. And Jennifer is glad that he did.

This is the house where Jennifer and Jake played basketball in the driveway growing up, and this is the house where they chased each other around the yard and had water balloon fights. And this is the house Jennifer ran to when her parents would fight and when she found out that they were getting a divorce. It's the only home of her childhood that's still in her life, and that's not something Jennifer wants to let go of.

"I've got to take a shower," Jake says, disgustingly eyeing his hands that are covered in a skin of pudding. "You good down here?"

"Of course."

"You know where the tea and everything is, so help yourself to anything, and your room is all made up."

"I know. I know," Jennifer says, playfully pushing on Jake's back to get him out of the kitchen where they're standing and into the shower where he wants to be. "I'll be fine."

Jake hustles upstairs to the shower, and Jennifer takes a mug from the cabinet. She knows her way around Jake's kitchen like it's her own -- the only difference being that Jake's kitchen is easily double the size of her kitchen. It's circular in shape with a large island in the middle of it that Jake built himself. It's a full butcher block, and she and Jake have sat around that kitchen island hundreds of times trying to piece together crimes or coming up with lesson ideas for Jennifer's second graders.

The island matches the butcher block countertops Jake installed on the cabinets that he refinished in a distressed white, at Jennifer's suggestion. Running to the bedroom that Jake always has fixed up for her, she passes through the family room where Jake's giant Christmas tree occupies the corner by the large windows that overlook his backyard.

When she gets into the bedroom, Jennifer throws her bag onto the navy duvet that's neatly tucked into the corners of the mahogany sleigh bed. She turns toward the dresser Jake has on the sidewall and opens the top drawer. That's where Jake's old t-shirts are.

Jennifer slips out of her sweater and into his grey t-shirt that says, "Michigan" across the front of it. Jake went to school at Michigan, but Jennifer slides some University of Iowa Hawkeye gear from her alma mater into his shirts every once in awhile. Stepping out of her jeans, she pulls on a pair of shorts, and then she hears the whistling of the teapot.

She grabs the book, her yarn, and her crochet hook from her bag and runs back into the kitchen.

With her ginger chamomile tea steeping, Jennifer snuggles into Jake's overstuffed grey couch that's angled across from the Christmas tree in his family room. Flipping on the tree lights, she feels an ease come over her. Jake's house smells like pine, his hardwood floors sparkle with glowing Christmas lights, and the puffy navy chair, his small cream rug, and the gas fireplace that has stockings hanging from it are all where they're supposed to be.

Finally Jennifer can breath and just relax. And that relaxation stays with her as she pulls the yarn onto her lap and continues crocheting Julie's baby-to-be's stocking that she started this morning, which now feels like days ago.

Her mind focuses in on counting stitches and rows as she moves into building the heel of the stocking and finishing at the toe. This is one of the things she loves about crocheting. It is the one time that her mind can shut off from the rest of the world and just focus on the present.

Putting in the final slip stitch and weaving in the loose ends, Jennifer evaluates her work. The stocking is a bit smaller than she imagined, but it's perfect for a baby's first Christmas, and her sister-in-law Julie is going to love the country "Father Christmas" feel Jennifer created with the maroon and grey yarn.

Jennifer's tea is almost empty, and she is starting to feel the chamomile pull on her eyelids. She thinks about curling up right here and pulling the soft fur blanket Jake has folded over the couch across her. She could simply fall asleep and forget all about the books, the murders, and what they still need to piece together to solve these crimes.

That dream is shattered, though, when Jake's voice comes booming from above her.

Jake's house has an upstairs loft that overlooks the family room, and Jake is standing right at the railing of it. "Do you know what I just realized?" Jake asks.

"That you take extremely long showers?" Jennifer playfully says as she tilts her head back and looks up at Jake.

"I had to soap three times," Jake says. "There was just so much pudding."

He turns away from the railing on the loft and runs down the stairs. He comes and plops right next to Jennifer on the couch. His dark hair is still wet, and he's wearing a pair of plaid pajama pants and a navy University of Michigan hoodie. Jennifer remembers when he got that hoodie his freshman year of college. It was right before he came and visited Jennifer in Chicago for Christmas break. She refused to go to Middlebridge like she usually did for the holidays because her dad had gone on radio silence. Jake decided to be the buffer, and he wore that exact hoodie every day when he visited her. Jennifer thinks about how strange it is that Jake looks the same as he did then -- his bright blue eyes are still unwrinkled, his body is still fit and strong, and his dark, black hair is just as thick as it was then -- yet, so much has changed around them.

"Matt Kealy lived in apartment 3C, right?" Jake asks, breaking Jennifer's observations.

"Right," Jennifer says, tucking her legs beneath her.

"And he had fourteen copies of *A Christmas Carol*."

Jennifer knows exactly where Jake's mind is going. It's the combination. The "33314." The Dickens novels weren't leading to Earl's apartment; they were leading to Matt's apartment -- third floor, apartment 3C, with "C" being the third letter in the alphabet and the third "3" in the combination. And he had 14 copies of *A Christmas Carol.*

That's why Fred sent Matt the plates, Jennifer thinks. The plates were a marker. A sign to whomever Fred was trying to communicate with to get this book. The plates would lead them to Matt's apartment building -- seeing as Matt's parking spot was outside the front of his building and visible to everyone -- and then the person would know to go to the third floor and apartment 3C. There they'd look for the 14th book of *A Christmas Carol*, which would be obvious since this copy matches the sets at both Fred's and Earl's place.

All of these pieces fuse together in Jennifer's mind with the speed of electricity, and she spews them out to Jake just as quickly.

He listens intently, loving the way her brain sparks and works, and when she's finished he says, "I think you're right," but then he pauses. He grabs the copy of *A Christmas Carol* and says, "But I also think that the five-letter number combination is an old army code."

"An army code?" Jennifer asks, not following at all.

"Let me show you," Jake says, opening the book to page three, paragraph three, and the third letter in that paragraph. He puts his finger on that letter, and looks at Jennifer triumphantly.

"You have to be kidding me," Jennifer says, as her eyes light up with the pattern Jake just revealed.

Chapter Seventeen

Christmas Cookies Begin

Jennifer stretches her arms and legs under the puffy duvet she snuggled under all night. It's still dark outside, seeing as time has just turned past 5:30 AM, but Jennifer's brain is wide awake as she remembers the discoveries they made last night, not to mention the new unanswered questions that kept them up until midnight.

The first number combination lead to the letter "e," but even more importantly, right above that letter "e" was another number combination: 172414. Following the same pattern they used for the first combination, Jake and Jennifer turned to page 1 and looked for paragraph 7, but there wasn't a paragraph 7 on page 1.

"The 172414 is 6 numbers instead of 5, which is how many were in the first combination," Jake said, trying to work through the new hurdle.

"And the last two numbers of both combinations is 14," Jennfer added.

"I think the '14' is a reference to the book," Jake said. "For some reason, this book is known as the 14th book."

"Okay," Jennfer said, "So then what we really want to look at are the numbers prior to the '14.'"

"We should put the 1 and 7 together," Jake said, quickly. "Go to page 17."

Page 17 was covered in dozens of number combinations, but Jake and Jennifer focused their eyes in on paragraph 2 and letter 4. It lead to a "b," and there was a new combination above that letter, and it ended in '14.'

They followed the number trail and flipped from page to page, writing down the combinations and the letters until they got to the last letter. It was an "e," and they knew it was the last letter because the number combination above that "e" ended in a 13 instead of a 14. The combination changed, signaling that their path had ended, and they were left with the message:

ebenezer's home

"Ebenezer's home," Jennifer quietly says to herself while still snuggling under the navy duvet. They didn't know what those words meant last night, and she still can't figure out their reference this morning. She knows that Ebenezer's home in *A Christmas Carol* is in London, but she can't even fathom hopping a plane to London with no clue other than "ebenezer's home" to guide her. And what are they supposed to look for in that home? Or is this an actual, literal reference to a home or some kind of metaphor?

Jennifer climbs out of bed, knowing that there's no way she'll be able to get back to sleep now that her brain has jump-started like a motorcycle race. She stretches her rested body that she can feel wants more than a handful of hours of sleep. She fantasizes about the possibility of a nap today, but she knows that dream is going to remain in fantasy land. They have too much to do. *She* has too much to do, and that's why she grabs her Ziploc full of cookie cutters and shuffles into Jake's kitchen.

She flips on the lights, puts on the tea kettle, and pulls out the flour, sugar, eggs, and other ingredients she needs for the Christmas cookies. She flies out for Chicago tomorrow, so there's no way she can delay making these cookies anymore. Luckily, she knew Jake would have all the ingredients; his kitchen is often better stocked than hers is.

Knowing that Jake won't be up for another hour, Jennifer figures this is the time she can dedicate to her to-do list, which was priority number one before the murders knocked that to-do list fully out of her mind.

Sipping her tea as she sifts the flour, sugar, and baking powder together in a bowl, Jennifer softly hums "O Christmas Tree" to herself as she thinks about the different shapes she'll form this dough into. Her mom always loves the Christmas tree cookies she makes -- the ones with the white icing and silver sprinkles that drape across the cookies like strands of silver ribbon. Her sister-in-law Julie always gravitates toward the candy cane cookies Jennifer meticulously ices with a combination of red and white icing, making sure to create strict divisions between the two colors. And her brother, Michael, never touches the cookies.

"I don't do sugar," he stubbornly says, and his wife Julie always beams at him with pride when he says this. She also then guiltily looks at her cookie and sets it down.

The oven beeps, letting Jennifer know that it's preheated to 350 degrees, and Jennifer is like a one-woman assembly line rolling out the dough, cutting it into shapes, and getting the cookie sheets filled.

The cookies only take seven minutes to bake, so by 6:00 AM, Jake's kitchen is filled with the smell of warm, baked dough.

Jennifer puts in the last batch of cookies as she piles another set on the cooling rack next to the stove.

She turns off the kitchen lights, wanting to only be by candlelight as the sun starts to come up. Feeling productive with these batches of cookies made, Jennifer decides she'll light the candles Jake has on his kitchen counter and get started on that tree skirt for Julie. It's a difficult crochet pattern, so Jennifer knows she'll need solid time working on it. Because Julie will expect it to be perfect.

When Jennifer is just about to strike a match to light the candles she's gathered, she sees something move outside Jake's back window. The object is swift and low to the ground. It also makes Jennifer's heart beat so vigorously that she can feel it in her ears.

At first she thinks it's an opossum or a big cat, but as her eyes focus in on the window, she sees that the figure is still there -- crouching down below Jake's window. Taking a silent, barefoot step closer, she sees a curve of a back. A human back.

Someone is crouched below the window, and it looks like they're digging something up in the bushes.

"This is the best smell to wake up to," Jake says, mozying into the kitchen. "But why are you in the dark?" he asks, reaching out for the kitchen light, but Jennifer runs and leaps on Jake before he has a chance to flip on the light. "What are you doing?" Jake asks, eyeing Jennifer like she's transformed into a rabid animal.

Silently, Jennifer points toward the window. At first Jake doesn't see anything, but then he sees the curved figure move. "What is that?" Jake asks, but then, a head pops up, and both Jake and Jennifer jump back. With the lights off, the person outside can't see them inside, but Jake and Jennifer intently watch as the person pulls a bundle of what looks like string from the pocket of their sweatshirt.

"What did he just pull out?" Jennifer whispers, eyeing the bundle.

"I don't know for sure," Jake says, "but none of this looks good." So even though he's in his pajamas, Jake swiftly heads to the front door, steps into his boots, opens the door, and disappears. Jennifer does the exact same, but she's a few steps behind Jake.

She follows his boot prints in the thin snow that stretches across the grass like cotton candy. When she gets to him, they both silently stand at the corner where the side and the back of the house meet.

There's a rustle, confirming that whomever was in Jake's bushes is *still* in Jake's bushes.

Jake looks over at Jennifer and mouths the words, "On three."

Jennifer nods and keeps her eyes on Jake's mouth as he holds up his fingers and mouths, "One. Two. Three."

Chapter Eighteen

The Boy Beneath the Window

The perpetrator below Jake's window immediately jumps into action when they surround him. Even though the sun is just starting to come up, they can see that he's wearing thick sweats. He has a hoodie pulled over his head, so they can't make out any specific facial features, but they can see that the man is fast and athletic.

But Jennifer is to his right and Jake to his left. He'll have to run through one of them in order to get away.

He chooses Jennifer.

But she's ready for him.

Even though the man is double her size and stealthy like a cheetah, Jennifer is quick-minded. She keeps her cool as the man takes his first and then second stride toward her, and just when he's about to zip past her, she sticks out her boot-covered leg.

The man trips right over it and tumbles to the ground. Jake quickly jumps on top of the man and pins his arms behind his back.

Jennifer proudly crosses her arms and nods her head, giving herself a second to gloat over bringing down someone almost twice her size. Although, she can't take full credit for this takedown. She learned all of her tripping tactics from monitoring second grade recess. Those kids may struggle with subtraction, but second graders sure do know how to trip someone.

The man wiggles and thrashes like a frightened worm, but Jake's weight and strength easily overpower the guy.

"Hold still," Jake says. "I don't want to cuff you, but I will if you don't stop fighting."

Jake doesn't have his cuffs on him, but the man must hear the confidence in Jake's voice because he quits struggling.

"Let's take him in the house," Jake says, keeping the guy's arms pinned behind him while he wrestles him to his feet. Jake looks at Jennifer to let her know he's good-to-go, and she leads the way. She keeps turning back to check on Jake and get a glance of the man's face, but his hoodie and the morning's darkness still hide his identity.

That is, until Jake gets the man inside, sits him down in a chair, and pulls back the hoodie. Jennifer flips on the lights at the exact same time, and that's when the man's face is revealed. But it's not a man that sits before them.

"You," Jake says, completely surprised to see the boy from the photo. "You're the kid I chased at Fred's house."

That's when Jennifer looks at the sweats the boy -- who looks to be no more than eighteen years old -- is wearing. They're the same dark grey sweats he had on at Fred's house two days ago, and now that his hoodie is down, Jennifer can see that he's also wearing the same black stocking cap.

His scraggly blonde hair that peeks out from his stocking cap looks riddled with dirt and grime. There's a film on his face that makes his skin shine like a greased pan. And his fingernails, which Jennifer sees when the boy crosses his arms and refuses to make eye contact with Jake, are jagged -- some of them broken down to the skin and some long and misshapen from neglect.

"Hey," Jake says, trying to meet the kid's eyes. "What were you doing outside my window?"

Even though the kid looks stubborn and tough with his straight, upturned nose and his crossed arms, Jennifer can see right through this act. What she sees sitting before her is a scared boy. And then she remembers the picture of him with Fred -- the one she found hidden beneath the stones of Fred's entryway. In that picture the boy was smiling. He was clean. He was hopeful.

Jennifer senses and fears that those photographic days and feelings are a memory long forgotten for this boy.

"Tell me your name," Jake says, leaning into the boy, but he remains silent.

Jennifer knows that he's going to remain silent if he feels threatened. That's why she steps in and says, "Would you like to take a shower and have some breakfast?" When Jennifer asks this, she's not sure who's more shocked -- Jake or the kid.

The boy looks up at her, and something in Jennifer's heart shifts into a crack. His blue eyes meet hers, and she can see that he's evaluating the truth and intentions behind her words, and when the boy senses that she's truly and earnestly offering him a warm shower and food, his tired, hungry and desperate voice says, "That would be nice."

"Come on, then," Jennifer says. She wants to reach out and put her hand on his shoulder, but she knows she can't push this too quickly. "Jake will get you some clean clothes," Jennifer says, nodding at Jake, who is still sitting in the chair baffled. "Right, Jake?"

"Uh," Jake throws up his hands. "Sure."

"I'm Jennifer, by the way," she says, holding out her hand to the boy.

He takes it and says, "People call me Junior."

Chapter Nineteen

Tight Lip Service

If there's one thing Junior can definitely do, it's eat. He's already had two helpings of eggs, six pieces of bacon, and he's currently devouring his third pancake that Jake just plopped on his plate. Yet, he's only using his mouth for eating, not talking.

Jennifer continues to eye Junior from the kitchen, trying to figure out how to break through this wall around him. She and Jake talked about tactics as Junior showered and the two of them got ready for the day, but neither one of them was prepared for his impenetrable armor of silence.

"So what's next on your plan?" Jake asks, joining Jennifer in the kitchen. "We going to buy him a car to try and get him to talk?"

Jennifer softly backhands Jake, but she also knows he's right. Junior has gotten a hot shower to rinse off his dirt; he's now wearing clean, crisp exercise pants, a Michigan t-shirt, and a thick pair of socks; and there's no way his stomach isn't reaching its maximum capacity with all the food he's consumed. It's time for him to give them something that they want -- like an explanation for why he was burning the books at Fred's house or why he was lurking around outside Jake's windows.

Jennifer walks right over to the table and sits in the seat next to Junior.

"So, you know Fred Gailey."

"Knew. I *knew* him," Junior says, but his words aren't soft or full of sadness like they should be for someone who just passed away. They're angry. Tight. Bitter.

"How did you know him?"

Junior looks out the window, not acknowledging her question or her eye contact. This act of avoidance isn't foreign to her; it's a common occurrence within the walls of second grade. That's why she takes the same tactic that she does with her students -- get them so emotional that they have to talk.

"I'm guessing that you broke into Fred's place. Were you there to steal things? Did you hear that he died and figured you would take what you could?" Jennifer asks.

Junior looks her dead in the eye, and she sees his jaw clench. "I would never do that. I owe Fred everything. I was there because he wanted me there."

"What do you mean?" Jennifer asks, hoping that Junior will continue.

"You wouldn't understand."

"Then explain it to me."

"Fred knew someone was after him. I know it," Junior says, shaking his head. "I got a letter from him just last week, and...I should have known something was wrong." Junior's eyes turn back to the window, and Jennifer can feel the blame that he's putting on himself.

"What did the letter say?" Jake asks, sitting on the other side of Junior, but Junior doesn't even acknowledge Jake's presence. "Look, Junior, we want to help. We want to find who did this to Fred--"

"You need to stop looking," Junior says, and that's when he turns his serious gaze straight on Jake.

"We're not going to do that," Jake responds.

"Then people are going to continue to die," Junior says. He stubbornly crosses his arms, but Jennifer sees his chin quiver. Someone or something has Junior terrified.

"Hey," Jennifer says, reaching out. Junior doesn't flinch or pull away when she puts her hand on his arm. "We're trying to stop people from getting hurt. We want to save lives, not endanger them."

"Then you'll stop investigating."

But Jennifer notices something. Junior's straight-forward words paired with his shaky voice don't match up. It's like someone else's words are moving across his lips. When he finally puts his eyes in line with Jennifer's, that's when she sees it. Junior thinks *he* is going to be the next victim. And then his blue eyes fill up with tears, which quickly roll down Junior's cheeks.

"Who has you scared?" Jennifer asks.

"No one scares me," Junior says, pretending that every bone in his body is full of toughness, but everyone at that table knows better.

"Then who did this to Fred?"

Junior wipes away the tears that roll down his cheeks. "I don't know. And then they got Earl, and--" Junior cuts himself off. Jennifer looks over at Jake, and his eyes grow as big a saucers.

"You know Earl?" Jake asks.

"He and Fred trained us."

"Trained you? Trained you in what?" Jennifer asks.

Junior takes the ends of his sweatshirt and presses the fabric against his eyes. Wiping away any excess tears, he looks at Jennifer and says, "It's easier if I just show you. Can you drive me somewhere?"

"Where?" Jake asks skeptically. He eyes Jennifer as if to warn her, *Don't you dare say yes until we know the details.*

"It's a place we call 'Ebenezer's Home,'" Junior says.

As soon as those words hit the air, there's no turning back.

"I'll get the keys," Jake says, not even needing to look at Jennifer to know that they're going.

Chapter Twenty

A Walk Down a Broken Path

Jennifer nervously checks the GPS again. She eyes the abandoned warehouses that line the street they're on and the industrial buildings that have white smoke billowing out of their chimneys. They're almost at their destination, which isn't exactly the news Jennifer wants to hear.

They've been driving for almost forty minutes, and even though she wants to know what's at this "Ebenezer's home," she does not like the look of this neighborhood -- with its broken sidewalks, grey air, and metal fences topped with barbed wire that line the properties.

Jake's car crunches over cinders and piles of soft slush. The snow here looks nothing like the snow in Middlebridge, which is puffy, white, and has a clean *crunch* to it. The snow in this place is like soupy ice cream with bits of grime and debris all mixed into it.

"So Fred and Earl ran The Society of Santas," Jake says, trying to get more out of Junior, who keeps backseat driving and contradicting the directions of the GPS.

"We call it the SOS," Junior says. "Take a right here, it's a shortcut."

"We're going to follow the GPS," Jennifer says, knowing that a shortcut is the last thing she and Jake want. They want time for more talking and more information.

"And you met Fred and Earl through the SOS," Jennifer says, summarizing the only piece of information Junior has really given them. So far, all they know is that Fred and Earl would go into boy's homes -- the kinds of boy's homes where boys without a home live -- but they don't know why or what it has to do with this "Society of Santas."

"Yeah, they came to The Academy," Junior says, leaning back in his seat when he sees that they're not going to take his shortcut suggestion.

Jennifer has heard about The Academy, but she's never known anyone who actually lived or worked there. It's the only orphanage, which everyone calls a "boy's home," in Wisconsin, and from what Jennifer knows, it's not state or federally funded, unlike most other schools in Wisconsin. It's fully run off private funds, and has been since the late 1800s, which means everything is kept behind closed doors.

"But the place we all call Ebenezer's Home is actually the headquarters for the SOS, but it's changed its focus...or purpose, I guess you could say…this last year."

"In what way?" Jennifer turns her head to look at Junior in the back seat.

"You know, Fred is the one who gave me my name," Junior says, changing the subject. He keeps doing this, which is beyond frustrating, but Jennifer can hear in his voice that this is a story he actually *wants* to tell, so she doesn't fight him.

"It's true," Junior says, meeting Jennifer's curious green eyes. "Cause, you see, when the SOS first started, Fred was helping us become Santas. You know, like at the mall and stuff."

"That's what the SOS was for?" Jake asks, looking at Junior from the rearview mirror.

"Yeah. Fred and Earl would go and help boys who didn't have a family learn how to be Santas." Junior looks out the window and then says, "Fred always said, 'Some people are born with a family and others go out and make their families.'" Junior pauses, and Jennifer's heart squeezes as she sees how much Fred meant to Junior.

"I bet you were a great Santa," Jennifer says, already seeing these pieces line up. Maybe Junior was a chip-off-the-old-block. Maybe Fred saw a lot of himself in Junior. Maybe that's why Fred gave him the name "Junior," and that made this kid feel part of something.

"You bet wrong," Junior says, laughing to himself. "I was the worst Santa. All those kids asking for toys they didn't need or wanting this dumb stuff when they already had everything that mattered in life irritated me," Junior says, shaking his head. "That's why Fred helped me do something different. Why we changed the SOS and it became Ebenzer's Home."

"*You have arrived at your destination,*" the woman's voice calls out from Jennifer's phone, halting their conversation. Jake parks on the open street. There's absolutely no one around, and the only sound is their car engine, which Jake turns off.

Jennifer looks up at the deep red building that's to the right of them. It's three stories tall, perfectly symmetrical with matching windows on each side, and it has a large green door in the middle. That door handles are wrapped in chains that come together with a thick lock.

Having the photos from Fred's house tucked in the inside cover of *A Christmas Carol,* she pulls them out and holds up the one of Fred and Junior. The backdrop in the photo is the same as the one she's viewing in person.

So the building in the photos is the SOS/Ebenezer's Home, Jennifer thinks. Although, she still doesn't know the difference between the two. She's about to ask Junior about this, but he already has the car door open.

"We have to go in through the back," he says, jumping out onto the sidewalk and walking toward a chain link fence.

When Jake and Jennifer head in his direction, they don't see a path to the back of the building. There's a long trail of busted concrete that's jaggedly thrown on top and next to each other. A few of the pieces have rusted spikes sticking up out of them. And, the "door" of the chain link fence has a thick chain around it, held together with a u-lock.

But when Junior gets to the "door" of the fence, he pulls the bottom part, and the metal fence bends open like it's made of rubber.

Jennifer looks over at Jake, who says, "This is looking more and more like a horrible idea," but he still moves toward Junior and ducks under the metal "door" that Junior is holding open for them.

The concrete wobbles and moves under their feet, and Jake holds onto Jennifer to keep her from slipping on the thin layer of snow that dusts the top of the concrete. With the dark clouds in the sky and the way the wind is starting to blow, Jake knows this snow dusting will turn to ice in under an hour. Junior, obviously knowing this treacherous path well, passes right by them and leads them down the side of the building.

The windows of the building are frosted glass. The lower row of windows have bars covering them, and Jennnifer can see that at least half of the top floor windows are broken. While the building is strong and resting on a solid foundation of brick and concrete, the rest of the place is completely neglected, including the dead grasses that are overgrown and brown.

"The door is right around here," Junior says, and as soon as they turn the corner, Jennifer almost gags. The stench of dog feces is everywhere. She covers her nose and mouth with the sleeve of her coat, and she sees that Jake is also sickened by the stench. Junior, however, doesn't seem phased in the least.

The entire back of the building is basically an open field that's gated in with a chain link fence; although, there's a section missing. And then Jennifer sees a dark van and a police squad car parked on the street behind the building. Not sure if these automobiles are abandoned like so much of this block, Jennifer squints to get a better view. But her concentration breaks when a large piece of wood smacks against some loose concrete.

"Sorry," Junior says, bending down. "It's not the best system to hide a key." He grabs a key from under the fallen piece of wood and starts fiddling with the lock. "This key is always tricky," he says, jiggling it back and forth.

Jennifer notices that a window at the far corner of the building is wide open. When she looks back to the squad car, it's like everything tunnels into clear view. If they open that door, they will not be alone.

"Wait," Jennifer tells Junior, but it's too late.

Junior throws open the door.

"Freeze," a voice says, but Jennifer can't focus on the voice. All she can focus on is the pair of guns that are pointed directly at her face.

Chapter Twenty-One

Little Pink Tongues

"Put your guns down," Jake says, stepping between the weapons and Jennifer.

"Lieutenant Hollow," one of the officers says in shock. "We didn't know you were coming. We heard a crash and some rustling, so we thought it might be the killer." The officer rambles off every excuse he can as he embarrassingly looks at Jake.

"Just lower your weapon," Jake says, now putting his hand on the young officer's gun. Jennifer would call this an "honest mistake," seeing that Jake isn't in his uniform. It's on its third wash and dry at Jake's house, so he has on dark jeans, his black boots, and a deep grey sweater under his black wool coat. But Jennifer's not convinced pulling a gun on anyone could ever fall into the "honest mistake" category.

"Sorry, Lieutenant Hollow," Officer Holtz says. Jennifer recognizes Officer Holtz, with her dishwater brown hair and sparkling hazel eyes, but she doesn't know the other officer, who casts his eyes down in shame.

Jake, Jennifer, and Junior step inside, almost slipping on the black and white tile floor that's cracked like peanut brittle. The scent of bleach and moldy towels lingers in the building, and when Jennifer looks to find the culprit of that smell, she sees Junior's face.

He's even paler than the stark, white walls behind him, and his eyes are wide with worry.

"What's going on here?" Jake inquisitively asks the officers, but Jennifer's concern is no longer on the officers in front of her. She moves next to Junior and puts her hand on his back.

"It's okay," she says.

Junior turns toward her, and she can see his panic glisten in his blue eyes. She's guessing cops make him nervous. She's also guessing that seeing cops in "Ebenezer's Home," which Junior basically claimed as his safe space, is only increasing his nervousness. And then Jennifer thnks about how Junior just lost Fred, possibly the only man who really looked out for him. She can't help but reach out and comfortingly say, "You're with us. You'll be alright."

Although his worried eyes don't change in the slightest, some color comes back to his cheeks.

Bark. Bark. Bark.

Jennifer's heart leaps, and she feels every muscle in Junior's back tense up when they hear the dogs' barks. Some of the barks are deep and mature, like that of an old, wise dog while other yips are full of excitement -- the kind of excitement only a puppy can find in life.

"Eb," Junior says, desperately looking at the doorway that connects this front room to the next room. And that's when Jennifer sees the small face of a yellow lab puppy peek around the corner of the door. He has a collar around his neck, and the leash that's attached to it is trying to pull the puppy back, which the puppy won't hear of it. He's too interested in smelling the door frame and then when he sees Junior, his little paws scurry in place.

He wants to run to Junior, but the leash is holding him back.

And then two more puppies, three adolescent dogs, and a pack of five full-grown dogs -- all different breeds from labs and retrievers to mutts with amber eyes and pink tongues -- come around the corner. What bonds all the dogs together though, is their barks, which echo and bounce off the walls.

But Junior raises his hand, and they all stop. Not only that, the dogs completely relax.

"Whose dogs are these?" Jake asks, reaching out and petting the golden retriever that's now resting against his leg. The retriever nuzzles into Jake's hand as he repeatedly strokes the shiny fur of the dog. Jennifer imagines that if that dog was a human, he would tell the best bedtime stories.

Jake crouches down, and Jennifer finds herself doing the exact same thing when the little yellow lab puppy Junior called "Eb," directs his big brown eyes on her. She doesn't think she's ever seen anything more adorable in her life, and she can't help but let out a small squeal of a "hi," as the puppy runs in place trying to get to her and Junior.

And then Captain Sharb comes around the corner.

He's at the end of the leashes holding the older dogs, and an officer Jennifer doesn't recognize quickly trails behind him. That officer is holding the younger dogs, and by coming into the room, he gives enough slack on the leashes to let little Eb run and pounce into Junior's arms.

Without even thinking about permission, Junior unhooks the leash and smiles as the puppy licks his neck, his face, and his ears. Then Eb angles his attention to Jennifer, and every part of her melts.

"Jennifer, meet Eb," Junior says. "That's short for Ebenezer."

Jennifer reaches out her hands and takes the little, warm puppy in her arms. When he licks her neck, it fills her with so much love that she feels like her bones are made of twigs. Eb wiggles and excitedly squirms until finally snuggling into the crook of her elbow. He looks up at her, licks his nose and then snuggles his face into her body and rests.

"Put that dog back on its leash," Sharb says, his bark harsher than anything these dogs could produce. "We're taking these dogs to the shelter."

"You can't do that," Junior says. "These are my dogs." Junior charges toward Sharb, ready to yank the leases right out of his hands, but Jake steps in.

Jake puts a hand on Junior's shoulder and quietly says, "I got this." The golden retriever moves to where Jake moved and resumes leaning his head and body on Jake's leg.

"What's the situation here?" Jake asks.

"These are your dogs?" Sharb asks, ignoring Jake's question and turning his beady eyes on Junior. "You have a permit for housing twelve dogs in a building that doesn't belong to you?"

"This building does belong to me," Junior says. "I know it does."

"No, this building belongs to Fred Gailey."

"What?" Jakes asks, and Jennifer can barely believe what she's hearing. Keeping Eb snuggled closely to her, she walks over to the others.

"What do you mean this building belongs to Fred Gailey?" she asks.

Sharb turns his authoritative and annoyed glare from Junior straight onto Jennifer.

"Look who it is," he says, his eyes narrowing at the sight of her. "I thought I told you to stay out of police business," Sharb says.

"So rounding up and stealing dogs who are happy, healthy, and in a safe home is police business now?" Junior sarcastically throws in Sharb's face. Then he turns to Jennifer. "This is what I wanted to show you. Fred helped me create "Ebenezer's Home." We train dogs to be service dogs and therapy dogs, but Fred handled all the paperwork, and since he died--"

"Save your story," Sharb says, cutting Junior off. "This place isn't registered as a shelter; you've got an entire kennel on the second floor without any permits; and I think you know what we need to talk about from this floor. You have some serious explaining to do, kid."

"You have some explaining to do," Junior yells back at Sharb. "Like how come you're spending your time going after innocent people and stealing their dogs when you should be finding criminals. Actual killers."

Jennifer sees Junior's face enflame as he throws these words at Sharb. Eb must sense Junior's anger too because his smooshed face pops up, and even though his puppy eyes are coated in sleepiness, he lets out a tiny *yip* in Junior's direction.

"It's alright, Eb. I'm alright." Junior reaches out and scratches Eb behind his ears, who licks the air as he does, and then turns those licks onto Jennifer's coat before nuzzling back down into his sleeping spot.

"You know, you're right," Sharb says to Junior. "We *should* be arresting some criminals," and with those words he hands the leashes to Officer Holtz and says, "Hold these."

He pulls out his cuffs, turns Junior around and starts reading him his rights.

"Jake," Jennifer yells, ready to get arrested herself to stop what's happening, but Jake holds up his hand. And Jennifer feels everything in her break when Sharb fully tightens the cuffs around a frightened and confused Junior.

Chapter Twenty-Two

The Back Rooms

Before Jennifer can do anything, everything has already happened. Junior is taken and shoved into the squad car that's parked out back, and the dogs are rounded up in the police van, including a protesting Eb who yips and yelps when he's taken from Jennifer's warm, loving arms.

His yips are nothing compared to the tearing Jennifer feels in her heart.

She wishes she could stop this. She wishes she knew what to say or what to do, but Sharb is the law, and she can't fight him; at least, not yet.

Sharb yells out to Officer Holtz, "Make sure you see them drive away." He points at Jake and Jennifer when he says this. "They are banned from that building."

Officer Holtz nods, and then turns around. "Shall we?" she asks, gesturing toward the yard behind the building, letting them know that she's going to follow Sharb's orders exactly.

"This isn't fair," Jennifer says, even though Jake is giving her a look to be patient. But how can she be patient after seeing those scared dogs piled into the back of a van and watching Junior be taken away without being given a chance to explain his side of the story? Plus, they still don't know how "Ebenezer's Home" fits into the message she and Jake decoded last night.

All of this sends her mind into a tailspin.

The three of them walk to the building, and Jennifer sees that the back door is still open. She imagines that Officer Holtz is going to lock it up for good right in front of their eyes.

"I could probably get fired for this," Holtz says, looking at Jake, "but go look in the back two rooms."

Jake stares at her with a furrowed brow and Jennifer does the same.

Holtz nervously looks over her shoulder, but when she sees that Sharb has already pulled away she adds, "Look, Sharb sent me back here to grab the camera he left and to make sure you two are locked out of here, so there's no time to be confused. Just go check out the back rooms while I take my sweet, sweet time getting the camera from the second floor."

In that instant, Jennifer falls in love with Officer Holtz. More than that, she falls in love with the way her hazel eyes twinkle at this deception. But, when Hotlz turns those twinkling eyes and her soft smile to Jake, Jennifer feels a different emotion; one she's not used to feeling.

And it inspires Jennifer to grab Jake by the hand and pull him away. He doesn't resist, so they quickly move through the front room, which they've already seen. When they enter the second room, though, they come to a dead stop.

It has the same black and white tile as the front room, but this room has five monstrous, black machines lining one of the walls.

"What are those?" Jennifer asks, but she answers her own question when she steps closer to the machines. She sees the block letters, the large roller that's covered in black ink, and the giant crank that's connected to a small conveyor.

"Printing presses," Jake says, putting his hand on one. "This one is warm," Jake says.

Jennifer feels what he feels and then puts her hand on the machine next to it. "So is this one." They check each of the machines, and all of them are warm. "Someone must have used this recently," Jennifer says.

"Yeah, like in the last day," Jake says. "But what for?" he asks, ready to investigate further, but then Officer Holtz comes into the room.

"Go to the two back rooms. We don't have a lot of time," Holtz says with a stern voice, "and you need to see what's back there." Holtz veers off to the right and takes the stairs up. Jake and Jennifer follow her orders and head into the next room.

It's completely dark. Jake turns on his phone flashlight, and it illuminates a dusty floor that has shards of broken glass and fallen debris on it. There are heavy, black curtains covering every window of the exterior wall. Jake's phone lights up the far corner of the room, which is piled up with large plastic containers.

"Those look like protein powder containers," Jake says as he and Jennifer move closer to the corner.

The containers don't have any stickers or labels on them, and they're all stark white. As they get closer they see that there's writing on the top of each container. There are four letters handwritten with a black sharpie.

"NaCN," Jake reads. He moves his light from container to container. "The same thing is written on all of these," he says. "What in the world is NaCN?"

"Na is sodium," Jennifer says, remembering the periodic table Mr. Schwank has hanging outside his sixth grade classroom. "But CN --"

"Cyanide," Jake says, giving her the other piece to the puzzle.

Jennifer feels chills move from her fingers to her toes. Both Fred and Earl were poisoned with cyanide. Jennifer crouches down and lifts one of the containers. "It's completely full," she says, looking up at Jake with worry.

"I've gotten the camera!" they hear Officer Holtz's yell from upstairs. "I'm going to be walking down the stairs soon!"

They don't have time to sift through their theories about these containers -- why they're here, what they were used for, and why Junior didn't tell them about this corner full of evidence. Jake quickly snaps a picture and says, "Come on."

He keeps his flashlight on and leads Jennifer toward the next room. The spotlight on the floor in front of them guides them past empty, overturned plastic containers, a broken broom, and empty garbage cans. The next room, which is the last room on this floor, is just as dark as the previous room.

The difference, though, is that this room doesn't have any walking space. It's filled -- from floor to ceiling and wall to wall -- with giant stacks of a greyish, white object.

Jake and Jennifer reach out and touch the stacks.

"It's paper," Jake says.

"Thick paper. Almost like cardboard," Jennifer adds.

"Are these all the same print out?" Jake asks. And without saying a word, Jennifer moves to the far side of the stacks, and Jake moves to the other side.

Both of them search for a piece of paper that's sticking out from the others -- one they can wrestle free. Jennifer finds a corner and wiggles the sheet free.

"I got one," she triumphantly says.

"Me too," Jake says.

They meet back in the middle, and both of them are speechless when their eyes fall on the design they hold in their hands.

The background is a grey-white, the ink is black, but most importantly, it's a flattened version of the pudding boxes they found in Fred's cabinet and in Earl's closet. The cyanide and the pudding printouts can only mean one thing: Jake and Jennifer are standing exactly where Fred and Earl's murderer stood.

And Junior has a key to this place, Jennifer thinks. *The place with cyanide and the pudding boxes.*

"This is why Sharb arrested Junior," Jake says. "Sharb may be a lot of things, but he's not a bad cop."

"There's no way Junior is the murderer," Jennifer says, shaking her head. "I can't believe that."

"Hey," Officer Holtz says, interrupting what would have soon become a debate. She peeks her head into the door frame. "Times up. And there's no way you can take those," she says, pointing to the printouts they're holding. "That's evidence."

Jake and Jennifer nod. They hand the print outs to Holtz and then both of them silently follow her out of the building.

Even though they don't say a word, their minds are racing. So Junior -- who was burning Fred's books that held a secret message, who ran away from Jake, and who was lurking around Jake's window before the sun was even up this morning -- claims that this building, which holds evidence linked with two murders and is owned by one of the victims, is his.

None of those details bode well for Junior.

But Jennifer can sense a criminal, and that's not the sense she gets from Junior. He loved Fred; she knows it. Although, then she remembers how Junior really didn't tell them anything about his relationship with Fred, except that Fred helped him "do something different."

What was this "something different"? Jennifer wonders. *Are Fred and Junior the shady characters in this story, and she's missed that fact? Did Junior blind her with his vulnerability?*

Jennifer runs her fingers through her hair, hoping that will stop the questions flying around in her mind. But nothing stops the wheels that are turning and churning in her brain.

For the first time in her life, Jennifer doesn't know who or what to believe. So after a quick goodbye and a thanks to Officer Holtz, Jennifer slips into Jake's car. Confused. Frustrated. And overrun with emotions.

Jake gets behind the driver's seat. "You want to go to Judy's?" he asks. "Talk this through."

Jennifer nods, not really able to live in the world of words quite yet. *None of this is adding up,* she thinks, but then she hears Jake's phone go off.

He clicks into it. "Text from my dad," Jake says. "He sent the receipt."

"The one from the bookstore? From Matt Kealy's parents?"

Jake nods as he opens the image.

Finally, Jennifer thinks, *a trail that might lead to some answers rather than this endless trail of questions.*

"Unbelievable," Jake says.

"What?"

"Look at the name of the place," he says, flashing his phone screen at her.

She leans in to see the picture of the receipt and at the very top of the image are the words: *Pelznickel Used Books.* Then she zooms in on the address.

"1450 Astor Street," she says in complete surprise. "That's close to my mom's place," she says looking up at Jake. But her look isn't just a look of surprise. It's one of determination.

"So no Judy's?" Jake asks.

"Nope," Jennifer says. "We're driving to Chicago, my friend."

Chapter Twenty-Three

The Dusty Corners of Pelznickel Used Books

The bell above the door jingles as Jake and Jennifer walk into Pelznickel Used Books. Jennifer stretches, having been crouched over in Jake's car crocheting the entire drive to Chicago. Julie's tree skirt is halfway finished, and Jennifer has the strawberry jam, the baby's stocking, the Christmas cookies, and the other presents all tucked safely in Jake's car. Plus, they're in Chicago. Cold, windy, feels-like-home, Chicago, which puts Jennifer ahead of schedule in one way.

She hasn't told her mom yet about this early arrival, but it's only three in the afternoon. Her mom won't even be at a phone until 6:00, so Jennifer decides she'll call her then. Even though this explanation is perfectly rationale, Jennifer still feels guilty.

It's not that she's avoiding her mom; rather, she's avoiding the avalanche of social events that always surround her mom. Jennifer can only take so many tea, lunch, dinner, and party dates.

Jake sneezes and pulls Jennifer back into the here and now.

"It's so dusty," Jake says, pulling a handkerchief from his back pocket. Jennifer also feels a tingle in her nose due to the dust that lives inside and around every crack and crevice of this bookstore. The creaky hardwood floors aren't helping, considering that they're covered in dozens of dust-filled rugs.

And, there are books everywhere.

It's not just the floor-to-ceiling dark wooden bookshelves, which wrap around every wall of the store, that are filled with books. Jennifer would expect that. It's that there are books stacked on the large puffy chairs that sits in the corner across from them. There are towers of books teetering in front of the overstuffed bookshelves. And the checkout counter, which is to the right of the front door and set right in front of the gallery window, has piles and piles of books stacked on it.

"Does anyone work here?" Jake asks.

As if hearing his queue, a fluffy orange and white cat leaps from behind the counter onto a pile of books. The cat has a bowtie for a collar, and it looks right at Jake and lets out a long *meooow*.

"You think he owns the place?" Jake asks. "Although, he's dressed a bit formal for this job," he says, cleverly smiling at Jennifer.

"Everyone makes that joke."

The voice that says those words is bland, monotone, and anything but amused. It's also hidden behind the fortress of books covering the countertop.

And then a rather unenthusiastic young girl -- maybe in her late teens or early twenties -- stands up. Her brown hair is dingy and jaggedly cut. Her eyes look tired with laziness, which is magnified by the large, circular wire glasses she's wearing. And her clothes are a collection of shabby colors layered on top of each other -- earthy browns, muted tans, dusty greys, and faded blacks.

"Hi," Jennifer says, walking over and reaching out her hand. "I'm Jennifer. Do you own this place?"

"No, I don't own this place," the girl says, greeting Jennifer's hand with a limp and emotionless shake. Then, under her breath she says, "Although, seeing as I've been left to do everything by myself the past couple of days, you'd think I did." Her words are quiet. Bitter. Angry.

"Is the owner here?" Jake asks.

"That would be me," an extremely jolly and rotund middle-aged man says. Jennifer looks at Jake to confirm that he just saw what she just saw -- that this middle-aged man literally emerged from the bookshelf.

"False walls," the man says when he sees their looks of disbelief. "Most of these open right up," he says, demonstrating by pulling open one of the few bookshelves that doesn't have a stack of books in front of it. It opens and reveals a small room that, not surprisingly, has more books in it. "Great for storage," the man says.

He closes the bookshelf and runs his hands through his thinning, grey hair. "So what can I do you for? Come to buy a last-minute Christmas gift? Better get it now because once we close up tonight at 5:00 we'll be closed for the holidays."

"Actually," Jake says, pulling out his phone as the man arranges the books piled on the front countertop, "we're here to ask you about a book you sold a little over a week ago. On December 14th, to be exact."

"We sell a lot of books," the man says, pulling his brown, wool sweater over his khaki pants. "I'm not sure I'll be able to remember the one you're asking about."

"This one is special," Jennifer says. "It's an old edition of *A Christmas Carol.*"

The man's hands freeze.

He stops arranging the books. He keeps his eyes diverted, so he doesn't have to look at Jake and Jennifer, but everything in his body goes into shock. And then, just as suddenly, he resumes his task of organizing the books.

"I'd remember if we sold that book," the man says, "and I haven't had a copy of *A Christmas Carol* in...well, I don't know how long."

The man is lying. Jake and Jennifer both know it. And Jennifer wants to know why this man is lying and why he's eyeing the girl behind the counter with a warning in his gaze. That girl crouches down among her castle of books and frantically looks from Jennifer to the shop owner.

She knows something. Jennifer can tell in the way her fingers fidget and her eyes jump around.

"Well, the purchasers have a receipt from your store," Jake says, showing the receipt to the man. "And it's for December 14. That is exactly nine days ago."

The man looks at the photo, but then he quickly shrugs. "I don't remember selling that book."

"How about you?" Jennifer asks the nervous, monotone girl behind the counter.

"Wendy wouldn't remember that," the shop owner says before the girl has a chance to answer. "She rings up hundreds of books a week. Isn't that right, Wendy?"

Wendy shamelessly hangs her head. She lets out a soft, "That's right," and she looks down at the ground when she does. A tension transfers between the shop owner and Wendy, which Jennifer knows is the cause for the girl's silence.

"Wendy is my niece. I'm doing her a big favor by having her work here, aren't I, Wendy?"

The girl's eyes fall to her brittle fingernails that have chipped blue nail polish on them. She puts one of those fingernails in her mouth and begins to chew. When she looks up at Jennifer and Jake, her eyes are the size of grapes, and they're as nervous as chattering teeth.

"You know, Jake, maybe we should get a gift for my mom while we're here." Jennifer says. "She's been going on and on about that Jane Austen book."

"Jane Austen," the shop owner belts out. "I've got any and every Jane Austen you could want."

Jake nods at Jennifer, knowing her exact motive.

"Where at?" Jake asks.

"Just follow me, young man." And they trail off to the far corner of the store where Jennifer knows Jake will keep this man occupied while she turns her attention to Wendy.

"You sold that copy of *A Christmas Carol,* didn't you?" Jennifer asks directly, knowing there's no time for preheating the conversation oven.

Wendy looks up at her, but her face doesn't soften or reveal information like Jennifer expected it to. In fact, she hardens, dead-eyeing Jennifer before she says, "You heard John. There's no way I could remember."

"Look," Jennifer says, glancing over her shoulder to check on Jake and John. When she sees that they're still occupied, she leans closer to Wendy, "two people have been murdered, and a young orphan boy has been falsely arrested. Knowing about the book could give us clues to help solve these crimes, so if you know anything, please tell us."

"What orphan boy?" For the first time, there's animation and life in Wendy's voice.

Jennifer knows the rules: she shouldn't disclose any specific information about the case, especially not to a perfect stranger. But Wendy is looking at Jennifer like she's on the edge of a verbal cliff.

She must somehow know Junior, which means she might help clear his name. So that's why Jennifer breaks the rules and says, "It's a boy named Junior."

A deep breath fills Wendy's chest. Her hands fly up and cover her mouth as she jumps to her feet. "Junior got arrested?" she asks, her voice too eager and too loud. It catches the attention of John, so Wendy pretends to pet the cat, who's sleeping on an open book.

"You know Junior?" Jennifer whispers.

"I can't talk to you here," Wendy says, and Jennifer hears a strain of desperation in her voice. Wendy is about to say more, but then she glances over at John, and her mouth snaps shut.

"Here," Jennifer says, quickly scribbling down her mom's address. "I'll be staying here and here's my phone number. Come by or call me anytime."

"I...I don't think I can," Wendy nervously says, and then John is upon them, having gotten the scent of their rebellious conversation. He quickly leads Jake back to the front.

The surprising part, though, is that Jake places a copy of *Mansfield Park* on the counter.

"Are you buying that?" Jennifer asks as Wendy tucks the note in her pocket and nervously rings up the book.

"I figured if I'm here I might as well get your mother a gift."

Jennifer smiles at Jake's announcement. No matter how much Eleanor despises him, Jake is always trying to win her affection. Or, at the very least, win some sort of approval. Jennifer doesn't have the heart to tell him that an old, hardback copy of *Mansfield Park* isn't going to do it for Eleanor.

"Fifty-two seventy-five," Wendy says, grabbing their attention.

"Whoa. What?" Jake asks.

"It's a great edition," John says. "Worth every penny," but even he doesn't sound convinced by this. In fact, he turns right around and starts frantically stacking more books in order to avoid Jake's skeptical glance.

"Well, it is Christmas," Jake says, handing the girl his credit card.

"Sorry, we're cash only," Wendy says, but then she gets busy handwriting what Jennifer imagines is the receipt. But that wouldn't make any sense. The receipt from Matt Kealy's parents was a printed one.

Wendy slips the paper inside the cover of *Mansfield Park* and throws a secretive glance at Jennifer.

"You know, I don't think I have fifty-three dollars in cash," Jake says, thumbing through his wallet.

"I do," Jennifer eagerly says, willing to pay hundreds of dollars to see what Wendy just slipped them inside that book. She and Jake pool their money together, and within minutes the book is in a bag, which gets transferred to their hands. They quickly say goodbye to Wendy and John.

"Come and see us again," John says, but his voice is tight, and his look is vicious when he turns it on Wendy.

The biting Chicago air pinches every part of Jake and Jennifer's skin when they step outside. "Fifty-two dollars for a book?" Jake asks, completely shocked. "I was wondering how that place stays in business, but now I know -- robbery by book." A dark layer of clouds have coated the sky like thick icing, so Jake and Jennifer hustle to the car.

Jennifer quickly glides into the passenger seat after Jake opens her door, and he hands her the bag. Without hesitating a second, Jennifer reaches in, grabs the book, and opens the cover.

"Does your mom even like Jane Austen?" Jake asks when he slips into the driver's seat. He blows on his hands to warm them up.

"Who cares," Jennifer says, holding the slip of paper from Wendy. "Look what Wendy left in the book." Jake eyes the handwritten note.

Go to Saks on Michigan Avenue. Ask for Alexa.

Before Jennifer even says a word, Jake has the car started and put into gear.

Chapter Twenty-Four

A Shopping Surprise

Even though Jennifer's mind is fully occupied trying to glue together the clues and the frustrations surrounding Fred's and Earl's murders -- not to mention how her heart continuously breaks whenever she thinks of Junior and the dogs, especially Eb -- she can't help but be taken in by the Christmas revelry of Chicago.

Even though it's just now four o'clock, the air has already turned a soothing grey, as if night never really left the city. The red and green stop lights shine like jewels, all the tree trunks are wrapped in white lights, and the street posts have glimmering wreaths and candy canes hanging from them.

As she and Jake walk from the parking garage down Michigan Avenue, there are shoppers rushing in and out of the rotating doors -- their hands filled with bags and their bodies covered in hats, scarves, and thick coats that button up to the neck. There's a group of carolers singing, "We Wish You a Merry Christmas" at the far corner of the street, and as Jake and Jennifer walk past Macy's window displays, Jennifer falls into the different storybook scenes that are decked out in Christmas themes.

"Look at this one," Jennifer enthusiastically says, running over to the window that frames Peter Rabbit and all his friends sitting around the fireplace -- reading books, drinking cocoa, and towered over by a Christmas tree draped in ornaments and flickering candles.

"Always a sucker for the bunnies," Jake says, playfully nudging her.

"They're just so cute with those ears," Jennifer says. She could stay and look at the window displays for hours, seeing as this was always a tradition that she and her mom did a few days before Christmas. That's when her mom does all her shopping -- loving the hustle and bustle and the efficiency of checking everything off her list all in one day.

"Come on," Jake says, turning a reluctant Jennifer away from the window display, "we need to go talk to this Alexa woman."

Within a few minutes, they've left the cold streets of Chicago and entered into the warm glow of Saks. The sound of the piano playing a jazz version of "Here Comes Santa Claus" from the second floor echoes throughout the entire store, which is showered in large silver and gold balls that sparkle against the lights of the cosmetic counters. A tree standing sixty or seventy feet tall is set right in the middle of the store, with large boxes of presents surrounding it on all sides.

The white lights, the trays full of hot chocolate for sampling, and the smell of cinnamon in the air, all warm Jennifer from the inside.

"Jennifer."

When she hears her name, all of that warmth inside Jennifer ices over. She's completely frozen.

"Jennifer."

The woman says her name again, and that's when Jennifer turns around and sees her mother.

"Jennifer, what are you doing here?" Eleanor asks.

David, her mother's driver, and Patrick, her mother's assistant stand next to Eleanor, their hands and arms dripping with shopping bags.

Her mom has on a pair of wide-legged, pinstripe trousers and a silky white button down shirt that's accented with a silver and diamond necklace. That necklace matches the diamond bracelet and diamond earrings that shine and sparkle under Saks' lights. Her blonde hair is cut bluntly at her chin, and her makeup accentuates her almond eyes and defined cheekbones.

"Mom," Jennifer says, feeling the word get stuck right in the middle of her throat. "Um, surprise," Jennifer says, throwing up her hands like all of this was planned.

"You aren't supposed to arrive until tomorrow." Eleanor says, narrowing her eyes at Jennifer, knowing that she's not telling her something.

"That's why this is a surprise." Jake says, stepping next to Jennifer.

Eleanor doesn't move when Jake says these words. She doesn't turn to Jake. She doesn't acknowledge Jake. Instead, she takes a few steps closer to Jennifer and fixes her hair.

"It's a wonderful surprise," her mother says, straightening Jennifer's peacoat and pinching a thread off of it. "You'll come to my party tonight."

"I, uh…" Jennifer wants to protest, but her mother is already putting plans in motion.

"Patrick," Eleanor says, "cross Jennifer off the list for calls to be made this evening. David, cancel the trip to the airport you had scheduled for tomorrow. And, Patrick, make sure Jennifer has a dress for the party tonight. I want it steamed and ready for her when she arrives home at seven o'clock this evening."

"Mom, I…" Jennifer tries to interrupt, but her mother washes those words away with more demands.

"I also want her room fixed up perfectly, and that includes having her tea ready for her arrival promptly at seven o'clock." It's no accident that Eleanor repeats the expected arrival time. Jennifer isn't being asked if she wants to arrive at seven, she's being *told* to arrive at seven.

Jennifer throws up her hands. "I guess I'll see you at seven." But then a small protest shoots up in Jennifer. Yes, she feels somewhat guilty about not telling her mom she arrived early in Chicago, but this is one of the reasons why. Her mother takes over her schedule and starts dictating every minute. That's why Jennifer stubbornly crosses her arms and says, "I'll only go to the party if Jake also comes."

Jake's mouth drops open like his jaw just detached at the hinges.

Eleanor turns and eyeballs Jake like he's a small rodent with dirty feet. She keeps her eyes on him as she says, "Patrick, we'll need to make sure this man has a proper suit for the party. He very well can't wear what he has on now." Her eyes move up and down Jake like he's a broken street light. "It's all settled then," her mom says, leaning in and kissing Jennifer. "I'll see you at seven."

And as quickly as she appeared, Eleanor turns and walks away. Patrick hands her the black, fur pashm cloak that Eleanor circles around her shoulders like it's a magician's cape. Jennifer's mom always wears these high-end ponchos, liking the drama of fabric spinning around her before it settles around her shoulders.

"I like this outfit," Jake says, looking down at her dark jeans and the button down shirt he has tucked under his grey sweater.

"Come on, Fashion Man," Jennifer says, "let's go find Alexa."

Chapter Twenty-Five

Turn up the Volume

"This feels very strange," Jennifer says, as she and Jake turn down another hallway. They're in what Jake has named the "intestines" of Saks. It's the basement level, away from all the glitz and glamour of the store, and it's where the offices are. Specifically, it's where Alexa's office is, according to the security guard they talked to.

"The security guard said room 14," Jennifer says, as they continue down the tile hallway that's completely empty and has minimal lighting. They walk past room 11, 12, 13, and when they get to 14, the door is closed. Jennifer knocks, and she hears the sound of high heels walking across tile.

The door swings open, and a woman in her mid-forties, who's easily six feet tall, greets them. She has blond, poofy hair that hits right at her shoulders. She's has an athletic build that she slims down in her black pantsuit.

"Can I help you?" the woman asks.

"Are you Alexa?" Jennifer asks.

"I am," she says.

"I'm Jennifer and this is Jake," Jake smiles and Alexa nods at them both. "We're investigating a case from Middlebridge, Wisconsin, and Wendy from Pelznickel Used Books sent us. We wanted to ask you about a copy of *A Christmas Carol* that--"

Before Jennifer can get another word out, Alexa abruptly gestures for Jennifer to stop talking. Jennifer obeys the non-verbal command. She's confused, but she still obeys.

Alexa steps into the hall and looks down the empty corridor before silently hustling Jake and Jennifer into her office.

She closes the door behind them.

The office is small, maybe eight feet by eight feet, and besides the desk that holds Alexa's computer and stacks of papers, there isn't much else to look at. Two chairs. A small shelf filled with supplies -- a box of staples, a dish of paper clips, and a cup of pens. Everything, though, is meticulously organized.

"Did anyone follow you?" Alexa asks, fiddling with her computer.

"No," Jake says, cautiously, "we weren't followed." He looks at Jennifer with a look that says: *Are we dealing with a nut case here?*

"If you're from Middlebridge then you know Fred and Earl? You know about their murders?"

Jennifer and Jake both look at Alexa in shock. How in the world does *she* know Fred and Earl and about their murders?

"Yes," Jake says. "We're investigating the murders."

Alexa gestures to the chairs on the opposite side of the desk, telling them to have a seat, and she turns her attention back to her computer. That's when Jennifer notices the door that's directly opposite of the door they came in. She wonders what in the world that back door could lead to, but then she's distracted by the Christmas music that Alexa puts on.

It's not the song itself -- "Grandma Got Ran Over By a Reindeer" -- that weirds Jennifer out; it's the fact that Alexa turns the computer speakers up so high that they'll have to strain their voices to talk.

Alexa takes a seat in her chair and rolls it over so all three of them are only inches apart. "What do you know so far?" Alexa asks, wide-eyed and straight to the point.

Jennifer and Jake look at each other, not knowing who this woman is, or if they can trust her. That's why they give her the bare information.

"We just know that a friend of ours bought a special copy of *A Christmas Carol--*"

"Leather bound with gold writing and gold-edged pages?" Alexa interrupts.

"Exactly," Jennifer says, now leaning in even closer.

"They bought the book about nine days ago," Jake continues, "but Wendy and John at the bookstore don't remember selling it to them."

Alexa lets out a sarcastic laugh. "You mean John won't let them remember."

"What do you mean?" Jennifer asks.

"Those books are nothing but bad luck."

"Books? You mean there's more than one?"

Alexa nods. "There are exactly fourteen books in that edition of *A Christmas Carol.*"

Jennifer's heart leaps and Jake adjusts in his seat. *Fourteen copies.* So they were right -- she and Jake have the 14th edition of the books, hence why the number combinations ending in "14" led them to the message in *their* particular book. That means there are thirteen other books out there and thirteen other parts to the message.

"Here's the story around those books," Alexa says, leaning further into Jennifer and Jake, who do the same. "They were given out to the men who played Santa Claus at Diamonts."

"What's Diamonts?" Jake asks.

"It was a department store," Jennifer says, remembering it well. Her mom told her about it going out of business just last year. "It was a huge department store. As big as these other ones."

"But Diamonts was locally owned." Alexa says. "By John's family."

"Wait," Jennifer stops her, "you mean John from the bookstore?"

"The exact one," Alexa says. "His name is John Diamont, and he's a terrible man. Don't let anyone tell you different. He's holding poor Wendy there like a prisoner."

"I thought he said he was doing her a favor by giving her that job," Jennifer says.

Alexa shakes her head. "John is Wendy's uncle, and when Wendy's dad discovered that she was going out with a boy he didn't approve of, he basically locked her up in that bookstore where John watches her all day like a hawk, and then her dad watches her all night. Wendy is trapped, and the poor girl is so depressed."

Jennifer can't disagree with that statement. Wendy's excitement for life was as drab as her clothes, which were deep earth tones of sadness.

"How do you know Wendy?"

"We're in school together. At the Art Institute. I met her last year when all of this drama started happening."

"Is she connected to Diamonts?" Jake asks, pulling out his notepad.

"Through family name only. Wendy's dad is a lawyer and was never interested in business, but her uncle John wanted to take over Diamonts."

"So John took over, and--"

"No, he never got the chance to take over," Alexa says, interrupting Jake. "John's dad, Robert -- who owned Diamonts -- he died about two years ago. And he didn't have a will; at least, not one that anyone could find, but I'll get to that," Alexa says, taking a breath. "So Diamonts sat in limbo month after month after month with lawyers and random family members all coming forward and saying that this person owned it, or that Diamonts rightfully belonged to this person." Alexa runs her hands through her hair. "It was a total mess. I was working at Diamonts during this time, but I knew it wouldn't last long. No one was managing the store because everyone was too busy arguing over who the store belonged to."

"How long did you work at Diamonts?" Jake asks, scribbling down every detail in the notepad.

"I worked there since I was a teenager, so a little over twenty years, up until they closed down. That's how I met Fred and Earl. They were both still Santas at Diamonts when I was in high school and working during holiday breaks."

Jake writes this down.

"Poor Fred and Earl," Alexa says, hanging her head. "They were the best Santas that store ever had, and they were such good men." She shakes her head. "I don't know if you know much about what they did, but Fred and Earl saved so many boys' lives."

"We know about the Society of Santas," Jennifer says, "but not the details of it."

"I don't know what's going to happen with those boys now," she says, "Robert, John's father, fully supported the SOS. But no else in the Diamont family is stepping up, and there's no way greedy John is going to take over the program. He's interested in money, not public service."

"Was John left anything when Robert passed?"

"That bookstore," Alexa says. "Robert, on his deathbed, verbally willed certain things to each of his kids. Wendy told me her dad, I think his name is Bob Jr., got a donation made in his name, her aunt got a house in the woods, and John got the bookstore. From the way Wendy tells it, no one was exactly thrilled with their gifts."

"Yet, John seemed happy when we saw him at the bookstore."

Alexa purses her lips. "If he's acting happy, then he's hiding something. That man is only interested in money, and that's not what the bookstore offers."

"I don't know," Jake says, "I paid over fifty dollars for a book there."

Alexa leans back in her chair and with a straight voice says, "I helped with Robert's financial books when he was alive, and Pelznickels *never* made a profit. But Robert loved that place. He adored books, especially the old-timey kinds of books that were hand-rolled and had thick pages with block lettering for the type."

Jake stops writing notes, and Jennifer knows he's thinking about what she's thinking about: the printing presses in Fred's building. Those presses could make the kind of old-timey books it sounds like Robert loved.

"That's why Robert had 14 special editions of *A Christmas Carol* made and hand-printed. He gave one to each of the thirteen men who played Santa at *Diamonts* throughout the years, like Fred and Earl, and he kept one book for himself."

"But neither Fred nor Earl had a copy of *A Christmas Carol* in their places," Jennifer says.

Jake gives Jennifer a cautious look, non-verbally reminding her that they don't know how trustworthy Alexa is. They still need to keep their discoveries close to their chests until they check out her story.

"The reason Fred and Earl were murdered is because of those books," Alexa says, her voice growing louder and eyes growing bigger. "It's rumored that those editions of *A Christmas Carol* hold Robert's will, so you can imagine how everyone is after them. Because Diamonts may be out of business, but that plot of land is worth millions of dollars. Anyone with one of those books is in danger."

Alexa takes a deep breath, closes her eyes, and then she stands up. She moves over to the far corner of her office, and crouches down. Jake and Jennifer eye her every move as "Up on the Rooftop" belts out from her computer speakers.

She wiggles a floor tile loose and there, sunken into a piece of wood below, is a combination lock. Alexa turns it this and that way and unlatches the wooden top of the floor. Reaching into the space below the floor, Alexa pulls out a book that sends chills all over Jennifer's body.

"I never wanted this," Alexa says, handing the copy of a red leather-bound *A Christmas Carol* to Jake. "Wendy gave it to me the first Christmas we met. Neither she nor I knew its significance then, but when we heard the rumors about the will just a few weeks ago, I locked it away, and we swore each other to secrecy. But I don't want this book, and if it helps bring Fred and Earl's murderer to justice, then I think you should have it."

Never before has Jake cared about books, but this edition of *A Christmas Carol* feels like it's made of pure gold.

"We can't thank you--" but Jennifer's words are cut off when a loud knock comes from Alexa's office door. Then, the door handle starts shaking and rotating with force.

"I thought you said you weren't followed," Alexa says, a quiver in her strained voice.

"No one was behind us," Jake says, but all of them are distracted with the jiggling doorknob. The door is locked, offering the person on the other side nothing but resistance. Then, they hear what sounds like a drill.

"We need to get out of here," Alexa says, grabbing her coat and quickly latching the chain lock. "That will only hold them for a bit."

She opens the door opposite the one the intruder is now drilling the lock out of.

"Follow me," Alexa says, and Jennifer and Jake don't look back as they all three step through the door and take off running down a dark tunnel without an end in sight.

Chapter Twenty-Six

A Tunnel Run

They run down the dark tunnel, lighting the way with their phones, for what seems like forever, but part of that is because Jennifer's heart is working double time -- pumping from the running and pumping from the adrenaline coursing through her body. When the tunnel comes to an end, it spills out into the lower level of the parking garage of Saks.

"We need to get out of here," Alexa says.

They didn't hear any feet behind them in the tunnel, but the intruder can't be far behind.

"Do you two have a safe place to go?" Alexa asks.

Jake and Jennifer nod, keeping their eyes on the tunnel that led them here.

"Then this is where we'll say our goodbyes." Alexa reaches out and grips each of their hands. "Good luck, and thank you," she says. "Fred and Earl were amazing men. They didn't deserve what happened to them, and they deserve to have their killer brought to justice."

The sound of quick-paced steps echo from the tunnel. They've run out of time.

Alexa splits off, hopping into her car and squealing out of the parking garage. Jennifer and Jake run toward the elevator, knowing that they need to get to the second floor and into the store. They can hide among the hoards of shoppers and then slip out and walk to their car.

That's exactly what they do, anxiously looking over their shoulders as they curve through batches of shoppers and weave their way back to the front of the store.

Somehow the Chicago air has gotten colder in the last hour, so it bites rather than pinches their skin when they walk outside. Jake and Jennifer bundle into their coats and Jennifer's boots click against the sidewalk like a fast-paced metronome. She's determined to get to Jake's car, open this book, and mentally organize all the pieces that just got added to these crimes.

As they're approaching Jake's car, his phone goes off. He furrows his brow at the number.

"Who is it?"

"I'm not sure," Jake says, picking it up and saying hello. He fumbles with the key fob, cradling the phone between his neck and shoulder, and finally gets the car unlocked. He and Jennifer slip inside and Jake turns on the ignition and puts the heat on full blast.

"Slow down. Slow down," Jake says to whomever is on the phone. "What do you mean you left?"

Jennifer looks over at Jake, whose eyes are large with worry. His hand is brushing up and down the dark scruff on his face that's grown in the last day.

"No, I'm not there," Jake says. "Jennifer and I are in Chicago, but you need to go back down to the station. Hello? Hello?"

Jake looks at his phone, but the caller is gone. He turns to Jennifer. "That was Junior. He ran away from the police station."

"What?" Jennifer asks, knowing that this is only going to cause more problems for Junior. "How?"

"I have no idea," Jake says, "but this isn't good. Junior kept rambling about how Sharb was going to 'put him away.' He said Sharb had all the evidence he needed to put him behind bars."

"You think that's true?" Jennifer asks.

Jake shrugs, but his voice is confident when he says, "Sharb may be a grumpy man, but he's a good cop. If he says he has the evidence he needs, then he does. He's not one to bluff."

Jennifer closes her eyes and shakes her head. "I can't believe that Junior is the murderer. There's no way he had any part of this."

"We can't know that for sure."

"I can," Jennifer says, defensively. "And if Fred put his trust in Junior...it just doesn't add up."

"I agree with that," Jake says. "Although..." Jake's voice trails off into his thoughts.

"What?" Jennifer asks.

"Fred and Earl were both poisoned, and to poison someone, you have to get close to them."

Jennifer shakes her head. She knows what Jake is saying, but she can't agree with the conclusion: That Fred and Earl both trusted Junior, so they'd have no problem eating food that Junior made, even if it was pudding laced with cyanide.

"Junior has no motive," Jennifer says, standing by her conviction. "It sounds like Fred and Earl were the only things keeping the SOS together, so why would Junior kill the system that helped and supported him?"

Jake's eyes fall to the book that's resting in Jennifer's lap. She opens the book, and, just like their brown-leather copy, this book has number combinations all over it. Every thick page is dotted and speckled in five, six, and seven letter codes -- each ending in a different two digit number between 01 and 14.

"How do we know where to start?" Jennifer asks out loud. She flips to the front of the book, and even though it has the Pelznickel sticker, there isn't a handwritten message like the one that guided them to an entry point of book 14.

"We need our book from the trunk," Jake says. "Remember how the last letter in our message of 'Ebenezer's Home' ended in a 13, which led us nowhere?"

"This is book 13," Jennifer enthusiastically says.

"We don't know for sure until we--"

Jake's words are cut off when Jennifer leaps into action and crawls into the back of Jake's car. She pulls down the black-fabric seat, and grabs the book she zipped in the top of her bag. She crawls back into the front, opens up the 14th edition of the book, and goes to the last letter in their message (page 105, paragraph 4, letter 9). She hands Jake the book Alexa gave to them.

"The combination above the 'e' is 234713," Jennifer says.

Jake flips to page 23, paragraph 4, and letter 7, but there's no combination above that letter. It's a dead end, which can only mean one thing.

"This isn't the 13th copy," Jake says, running his hands through his hair. "Basically, we have to have all fourteen copies of the books in order to decipher the code," Jake says, his eyes twinkling with a plan.

"What are you thinking?" Jennifer asks.

Jake turns in his seat so he's fully facing her. "If Wendy, who works at Pelznickels, gave this book to Alexa, and Matt Kealy's parents somehow bought a different edition of the same book from Pelznickels, then all signs point to one place."

Pelznickels, Jennifer thinks.

Jake looks at the clock in his car. It's 5:03.

"What time did John say the bookshop was closing?" Jake asks.

"5:00," Jennifer says. "And he said that they'd be closed for the holidays."

Jake picks up his phone and starts dialing.

"Who are you calling?" Jennifer asks

"I'm calling in a favor from the Chicago PD," Jake says. "But this is going to take a miracle, so I hope you haven't used your Christmas wish yet."

Chapter Twenty-Seven

Behind the Bookcase

Just as John said, Pelznickels is locked up and shut down for the holiday season -- no lights on, no movement inside, and a curtain pulled down over the main door, which has glass inlay framed in green-painted trim. The gallery window -- which is next to the main door and has the name Pelznickel Used Books stenciled in gold letters that curve across the glass -- isn't covered, so Jake keeps peering into the shop as they wait.

The cold, slicing air of Chicago has softened and small, white snowflakes start to fall from the sky. The powdery flakes land on Jennifer's black boots, and they melt into liquid before waterfalling off the side of her boots.

They've been waiting outside the bookstore for almost twenty minutes. In those twenty minutes, Jake has assured Jennifer hundreds of times that his contact, Erin, is going to come through. But now that time is ticking close to six o'clock, Jennifer has a different stress on her.

She has to be at her mother's by seven o'clock. She's already on thin ice with her mom, and if she doesn't show up at seven, that ice is going to crack, and Jennifer is going to fall straight through it.

"There she is," Jake says, his eyes lighting up.

Jennifer follows the direction of Jake's view, and she sees a tall, maybe around 5'7", brunette woman -- in her mid-to-late forties -- taking long, lean strides toward them. She has on black boots with a tall heel and her black, wool coat is accented with a red and grey plaid scarf.

She's pretty, Jennifer thinks. But as the woman gets closer, and her wavy hair and creamy flawless skin come more into view, Jennifer changes her sentiments.

No, she's gorgeous, Jennifer thinks.

Jennifer looks over at Jake, whose eyes have glossed over with a film of awe. He straightens his coat and clears his throat. Jennifer side-eyes him, and a mischievous smile comes to her lips.

"What?" Jake asks, a nervous quiver in his voice. "She's a colleague. And my superior." Jennifer isn't buying that those two facts are the reason for Jake's fidgeting.

"So this is what it takes to get you to call me, huh?" The woman says when she reaches them. She's not smiling, and she looks like a superhero with the way she has her hands on her hips, her shoulders rolled back, and her legs hip-width apart. Jennifer feels an unexpected tension grow as this woman, Erin, stares right at Jake.

But then, Erin's serious face breaks into a friendly smile with lit-up eyes and rosy cheeks. "You know I'm just playing with you," she says, slugging Jake in the arm. "How are you, Jakey?" She and Jake embrace in a familiar and comforting hug.

"I'm good," Jake says.

"And what about my favorite mom and dad?" she asks. "How are Carol and Jefferson?"

"My parents are good. The whole family is good." Jake says.

Then, Erin turns her attention to Jennifer, who it seems Jake has forgotten is standing right next to him.

"Oh, this is my friend Jennifer," Jake says. "She's helping me out with the case."

"Finally I get to meet her in the flesh," the woman says, holding out her black-leather gloved hand to Jennifer. "I'm Erin, and I've heard so much about you."

"Nice to meet you," Jennifer says, shaking her hand and wishing she could say the same about this mystery girl that Jake has never told her about.

"So, did you get it?" Jake asks, eagerly looking at Erin's purse.

"Do I ever disappoint?" she asks, and from her oversized black purse she pulls out the piece of paper that makes Jake throw his hands up in celebration. It's a warrant to search the property of Pelznickel Used Books. "I also brought my friend along," Erin says, pulling out a small plastic case.

She opens it up, and all Jennifer sees are slivers of thin metal -- different sizes with varying curves and angles. Erin moves past Jennifer and Jake and puts her bag down on the concrete. She squats and crouches down until she's eye level with the locks on the front door of Pelznickels. With a confident smile, she looks over her shoulder at Jake and says, "You going to time me?"

"Obviously," Jake says, looking at his watch.

And then Erin gets to work -- sticking this and that metal piece or curved rod into a lock until she can turn it with ease. She gets the two top bolts opened in no time, but the lower lock is giving her resistance. She jiggles the doorknob while turning the two metal sticks this and that way. "Come on," she says, and just like that, the doorknob fully turns.

"Done," she yells, throwing her hands up like it's the end of a test.

"One minute and seventeen seconds," Jake says.

Erin sighs. "I'm slowing down in my old age." She pushes the door open, and they all step into the warmth of the bookstore.

The bell above the door jingles as they shut the door, and Jennifer half expects the orange tabby cat with the bowtie to jump up and greet them. But nothing in the store moves or stirs. Not able to find the overhead light switch, Erin clicks on the small lamp that's sitting on the front counter, which is still covered in piles of books.

The light bulb illuminates a golden, warm glow, and when Jake clicks on a lamp that's on one of the bookshelves, the store almost glimmers. Even though Jennifer knows she's in the same store she was in just a couple of hours ago, something about it is different. Without the depressed Wendy, the glaring John, and the fluorescent overhead lights, this place resonates nothing but cozy charm.

Jennifer starts to get a sense of John's father as she looks around at the thick volumes of books and the puffy chairs that ask someone to stop, curl up with a book, and disappear to a new place.

"What exactly are we looking for here?" Erin asks, taking off her coat and gloves. She has on a black v-neck sweater that hits right at the top of her jeans. Jennifer does the same, taking off her coat and letting her cream, long cashmere sweater drape over her black leggings.

"We're looking for a set of books," Jake says.

Erin angles her head. "You're kidding me, right?" she asks.

"They're a special set of books," Jake says. He gestures to Jennifer's bag, and she hands him the two copies of *A Christmas Carol* -- one from Matt Kealy's place and the one Alexa just gave them.

As Jake tells the story behind the books to Erin, Jennifer pokes around the bookstore. She peeks into some of the old texts that are lying in stacks on the floor. There are books of poetry, a graphic novel from the early 1900s, and when she stumbles upon an old set of Winnie the Pooh books, she can't help but pull one out.

Her dad used to read her these books every night when she was young -- the two of them laughing over Tigger and feeling sorry for sad, depressed Eeyore. Jennifer opens the book and runs her hand across the page. When she does, those memories of her and her dad flood over her. At first the memories are warm and comforting, but then she thinks about how her dad is no longer in her life. She thinks about the fact that he simply disappeared, so just as drastically, she snaps the book shut and tosses it back on the pile where she found it.

Feeling a shift in her, Jennifer focuses on the task at hand. She eyes every book she passes, looking for any leather-bound books with gold writing. There are many, but none of them say *A Christmas Carol* on them. Jake, Jennifer, and Erin all take different sections of the bookstore, but after almost thirty minutes, they come up with nothing.

Jennifer looks at her watch. They need to leave in ten minutes if they're going to make it to her mother's place by seven. Maybe they could come back tomorrow. Although, they've looked through almost every bookshelf.

The false walls, Jennifer thinks. "The walls," she says. "We need to pull out the walls."

"Is she okay?" Erin asks, looking at Jennifer like she's let all her screws loose.

"Right," Jake says, looking at Jennifer. He goes over to a bookcase and pulls on it. It doesn't move. He pulls again. It still doesn't move.

"Actually, are *you* alright?" Erin asks, skeptically eyeing Jake.

"Some of these open," Jennifer explains, seeing that Erin thinks they're both insane. Jennifer walks over to one of the bookcases, and when she pulls, it easily opens. Behind it is a bunch of brooms, buckets, cleaners, and a vacuum that looks as old as some of these very dusty books.

"We should only focus on the bookcases that have stacks of books in front of them," Jake says, already getting to work removing the books. "The ones that look like no one wants them to be opened."

And that's exactly what they do, hauling and moving the books that stand guard in front of certain bookcases.

The first case they clear doesn't budge. Erin is working on the second one as Jake and Jennifer join forces on the one across the room.

Erin gets her bookcase cleared, and when she pulls on the shelf, the whole case creaks open. There's some resistance in the hinges, but she muscles it until the small light in the store can penetrate the darkness behind the shelves.

"Uh, guys," Erin says to Jake and Jennifer, who are busily moving stacks of books here and there. "I think you should come look at this."

Jake and Jennifer drop the books they're holding, and they run over to Erin.

"Are you seeing what I'm seeing?" Erin asks, lighting up her phone and pointing it at the large object in front of her. "Or have I just lost my mind?"

Chapter Twenty-Eight

The Book Launch

Behind the bookcase is a safe. A dark, steel safe that easily stands four feet tall and three feet wide. More than that, it is covered in chains, and each of those chains has a thick lock on the end of it. Although Erin is looking at this safe with her lock-picking brain on, all Jennifer can see is Earl.

When they found Earl dead in his apartment, he was covered in chains just like this safe is, and she can't think that is a mere coincidence.

"Can you get through those locks?" Jake asks Erin.

"Give me some light," Erin says.

Jake and Jennifer spotlight her with their phone flashlights, and Erin gets to work sticking this and that metal sliver into the locks until they unlatch. Although she busts open lock after lock in record time, Jennifer knows that it's not fast enough. She has to get to her mother's, and at this pace, she's definitely going to be late. But then she stops herself. *I'm on the brink of solving murders, and I'm*

worried about arriving on time so I can attend a party that I don't
even really want to go to.

And that settles it. Jennifer turns her phone around, and dials her mom's number.

"I need that light," Erin says.

"Sorry," Jennifer says, "this will only take a second." Jake covers for Jennifer by stepping closer to Erin in order to give her more direct lighting.

Jennifer's mom doesn't answer the phone -- she's most likely getting ready for the party -- but her assistant Patrick does.

"Just tell my mom that we're running late, but we'll be there as soon as possible," Jennifer says.

Patrick doesn't argue, but Jennifer can hear the warning in his voice when he says, "Alright, I'll tell her."

Feeling slightly relieved, Jennifer hangs up and shines her phone light back on Erin's work.

Click.

The last lock opens, and the chains fall off the safe like a dress that's four sizes too big. Erin grips the safe's handle, pulls it down, and the door creaks open.

"Jackpot," Erin says when she opens the door and reveals the stack of books.

"No way," Jennifer says, feeling like this is a trick.

"Are there twelve books?" Jake asks, quickly eyeballing the different colored books that are perfectly stacked on top of each other.

Erin, who is still crouched down by the safe counts them. "Twelve copies of *A Christmas Carol*," Erin says, looking up at Jake. "I told you I never disappoint."

"I'll grab our two books," Jennifer says. "Then we can decipher the message." She quickly pops up and runs over to the front counter where she left them.

"I can't believe we found them," Jake says, watching as Erin stacks all of them in her arms. "Now all we need to do is decode--"

Thwack.

A thick hardback book hits the wall closest to Jake and then lands on the floor with a *thud*.

Jennifer spins around when she hears the sound, and in the shadows of the light she sees John, the jolly bookstore owner from earlier. But the hateful hunch in his back and his vengeful eyes, which seem to glow fire as he moves closer to Jake and Erin, are anything but jolly. John has a stack of books in his arms -- heavy, hardback books -- that Jennifer can see he plans to use as weapons.

Behind John, Jennifer also sees an open bookcase, but it's not one they opened. It has a staircase behind it, which is obviously how John is standing in front of them, ready to battle them with books.

"What in the--" Jake doesn't get another word out. As soon as he turns around to assess what just happened, he's greeted with a hardback book, and this one hits him square in the face. "Ow," Jake yells, bending over and cradling his face in his hands.

"Jake," Jennifer yells, dropping the books she retrieved and running to his side.

"Thieves! You're thieves!" John yells. "Those books are mine!"

"Sir, I'm Chicago PD, and you need to drop the books you're holding and put your hands up," Erin says to John, but his wily eyes show that he's not listening to a word she's saying.

Erin stands up -- still cradling the set of *A Christmas Carol* books she took from the safe -- and steps out of the small area tucked behind the bookcase. "Sir, I'm going to go get my badge that's in my bag," she says, "you need to stay still."

But before she can finish her first step, John launches a book straight at her head. She drops the editions of *A Christmas Carol* she's holding and blocks the book-turned-weapon with her arms just in time.

"You think you can take away my business?" John yells. "You think you can steal what is now rightfully mine?" John's eyes are wild, he's breathing out of his nose like a bull, and his face is blistering red. "Those are my books! You're the thieves!" He's yelling these words, and they screech across his throat.

John whips another book at Erin, like it's a frisbee, and it hits her square in the stomach. Erin hunches over, but then she snaps back up, and when she does, it's like she turns into a wild animal. She charges straight for John, who tries to throw another book at her, but Erin leaps on John before he gets the chance.

Jake, ignoring the pain caused by the book-straight-to-the-face situation, sees Erin tackle John down to the ground. They're wrestling back and forth. Jake jumps into the action, sprinting over to them and pinning his knee right in the middle of John's back. Then, he grabs John's arms and anchors them to his lower back.

"I don't have my cuffs," Jake says, looking at Erin, whose hair is like a bird's nest after wrestling with John. She jumps up, seeing that Jake can easily hold John himself, and she runs over to her bag. She returns to Jake within seconds and says, "Like I said, I never disappoint." She displays a bundle of zip ties like they're a winning hand in cards.

With John's wrists and ankles zipped together, Jake flips John onto his back.

"You don't understand," John says, his voice having changed from yelling to whimpering. "Those books are mine! You can't do this to me! I won't let you do this to me!"

"You have the right to remain silent--" Erin tries to say.

But John mutes her words with his continuous yelling of, "You can't take them. He gave them to me. Ebenezer gave me those books."

Erin looks at Jake, who looks at Jennifer, and they're all thinking the same thing: *John has gone mad.*

"Ebenezer wanted me to have these books," John yells again.

"We need to get him to the station," Jake says, his voice calm. "Sir, we're going to take you to the station."

"But Ebenezer…" John's voice trails off as he breaks into tears.

"My car is maybe a block away," Erin says.

Jake looks over at Jennifer, but Jennifer's eyes are on the man she sees breaking down right before her. But, then, her eyes drift to the staircase that is hidden behind the bookcase -- the one John secretly came down. All of her instincts tell her to follow those stairs.

"You alright if I take him out to Erin's car with her?" Jake asks Jennfier.

Jennifer nods, turning her attention to Jake. That's when she sees the red bump forming on Jake's forehead. It has a small cut from where the edge of the book got him.

But before she can say something or show her concern, Jake has John on his feet, and looks over his shoulder as he tells Jennifer, "I'll be right back. Lock the door behind us."

Jennifer does exactly that, but then she takes off running and goes up the pokey staircase to see where it leads.

Chapter Twenty-Nine

A Not-so-Normal Hobby

The stairs are enclosed on all sides. The walls are painted a deep maroon, and there's a single candlestick sconce domed in glass that lights the way up the wooden steps. The flame flickers and casts a deep shadow as Jennifer walks by it. When she gets to the top of the stairs, she finds herself in a room that has two large windows on the far wall that frame the twinkling lights of the city.

The walls of the room are covered in paneling that's painted a light green. There's an iron bed in the corner of the room, and the white, crumpled sheets are pulled back as if someone hurriedly jumped out of bed. Taking a few steps in, the hardwood floor creaks under her feet. There's a winged armchair opposite the bed, and next to it is a side table stacked with books and a lamp that glows warmly throughout the room. The chair is angled by a crumbly, red-brick fireplace that has two crackling logs wrapped in flames.

As Jennifer walks further into the room, she smells an unfitting stench -- like alcohol, or ammonia, or a liquid that she can't name but can feel bothering her nose. She follows the smell, and it leads her to a door that's next to the staircase. She sees a small kitchen off to the side of the door, but her true interest lies with what's behind this door.

She opens it, and when she does, the stench crashes on her like a wave. She covers her nose and mouth with the sleeve of her cream sweater.

"What is that smell?" she asks, feeling for and finding a light switch on the wall.

When the room, which must have originally been a walk-in closet, is flooded with light, Jennifer sees the culprit for the stink. There are mounds and mounds of mooshy, pulverized paper covering the long table that's in the middle of the room. The table has a red cloth covering and draping off the sides of it, which makes no sense to Jennifer, seeing as this damp paper is on top of it.

There is a stainless steel machine that looks like a hollow torpedo to her right, and it's dripping with remnants of milky water and pulverized paper.

What is he making? Jennifer wonders, having no idea what John is up to. She continues to walk through the room, getting to the end of the long table. There in the back, sitting on the floor, are three small stacks of paper, but this paper isn't like normal paper.

It's heavier; it's yellowed rather than white; and she can actually feel the fibers when she touches it. And, this paper feels exactly like how the thick pages of the *A Christmas Carol* books feel.

Jennifer's heart stops, though, when her eyes land on the plastic container that's lodged behind those stacks of paper. It's exactly like the containers they saw at Fred Gailey's building, and just like those, this container also has the letters NaCN written on the top -- in the same black-marker handwriting.

She needs to see Jake's photos to be sure, but Jennifer is convinced that this isn't just a container that's *like* the ones at Fred's building. This container is *from* Fred's building.

"So John has the *A Christmas Carol* books and a container full of cyanide," Jennifer says, feeling the evidence stack up against him. "Now all we need is to find some pudding mix," she says, but her gut tells her that they've found their murderer.

She picks up the container of NaCN, wanting to know how much is left, and when she does, she feels a piece of paper on the back of it.

Turning the container around, she sees a folded letter stuck to the back side. She pulls it free, opens it, and her eyes zoom across the words on the page. But, it's the signature at the bottom that catches her eye.

"Fred Gailey," she says, reading the signature out loud. The letter is a notification to John Diamont, informing him that the Gailey Press, while having loved and respected their decades of business with Robert Diamont, will not be continuing their services with John. "We regret that your intentions for the duplication of the *A Christmas Carol* novels made by your father, Robert Diamont, do not correspond with the mission Robert stood for, or what this press stands for." Jennifer reads that last line of the letter out loud.

Then she looks at the top. The date in the right-hand corner is from one year ago.

Boom. Boom. Boom.

The fist banging on the door downstairs echoes through the store and up the stairs, and it sends Jennifer's heart pounding like the inside of a speaker.

"Jennifer," she hears Jake's strained voice yelling from outside. She keeps hold of the letter from Fred and sprints back down the stairs.

Jake is peering into the portrait window at the front of the store like a hungry animal in search of warmth and food. When he sees Jennifer come into view, he moves right in front of the main door, which she unlocks and opens.

"Where were you?" Jake asks, quickly moving into the store and rubbing his hands together to warm them up.

"I went up that staircase, and Jake, look at this." She hands him the letter. As he reads it, she can't stop herself from saying, "John has some sort of paper-making situation going on upstairs. And, he has a container of cyanide."

She expects Jake to look at her with surprise when she says this, in a "Eureka" kind of moment, but when he finishes the letter, he folds it back up and says, "So it all fits together."

"Wait, what all fits together?" Jennifer asks, feeling like she's missing something.

"John never stopped yelling about those books. He screamed every second as we took him to Erin's car about how those books are his new chance. Yelling about how they are the inheritance he deserves."

"Do you think the rumors are true?" Jennifer asks. "Do you think the books hold a message to Robert's will."

"Yes," Jake says.

Although he stands still, Jennifer immediately runs over to the copies of *A Christmas Carol* Erin dropped. She gathers all of them up, ready to follow the text trail Robert left.

"But I don't think it's Robert's will that John is after." When Jake says this, Jennifer looks up at him.

"What do you mean? What else would he be after?"

Jake furrows his eyebrows as he thinks this through out loud. "I don't think John wants whatever is at the end of the message in those books. In fact, I have a sneaking suspicion he wanted to stop anyone from ever piecing the message together. Hence the hiding of the books." A glimmer of excitement covers Jake's eyes as he says, "Which is why we should decode that message right now."

He doesn't have to tell Jennifer twice.

They both lug the *A Christmas Carol* books over to the front counter, but it's already covered in books, so Jennifer sets down her stack, rolls up her sleeves, and then swipes her arms straight across the counter -- sending every single book that was piled up there flying off the counter and onto the floor.

Jake looks at her like she just grew a second head.

"What?" Jennifer says with a shrug. "We need a place to lay out all the books." And without giving Jake's look of wonder a second thought, they line up all fourteen copies of *A Christmas Carol* on top of the wooden counter. Each one is a different color -- from deep orange and eggplant purple to festive green and cherry red.

"What was our last number combination from book 14?" he asks.

"234713," Jennifer says, having committed that number to memory. Both of them get to work, turning to page 23 in every copy of the books they have in front of them. Then, they go to paragraph 4 and to the 7th letter. If that 7th letter doesn't have a combination ending in 13 above it, then they know they're not in the 13th edition of the book. They go through book after book, each time hitting a dead end.

"I got it," Jake says. "Look," and he shows Jennifer how the 234713, leads to an "L" in the book he's holding. And the "L" has the combination "994313" above it. "See how the 994313 also ends in 13?" Jake asks, quickly flipping to page 99, paragraph 4, and letter 3. It's leads to an "e" and above that letter is the combination "4523413."

"So this is book 13," Jennifer says.

"Now we keep following the numbers and letters," Jake says. They flip, and read, and write down the letters that the numbers lead them to, each time organizing the books so they're in order -- from edition 01 to edition 14. They go from page to page, paragraph to paragraph, and letter to letter, each combination directing them to a letter of the message. Until finally, they have the full message:

My Will and Testament Can Be Found On The Pudding Package I Left At Ebenezer's Home.

"The pudding package?" Jake asks. "You mean those thousands and thousands of printed pudding packages in Fred's building have Robert Diamont's will and testament on them?"

Jennifer remembers how those stacks of printouts reached from floor to ceiling and from wall to wall in that back room of Fred's building. "Do we seriously have to search through every one of those pudding printouts?" she asks.

A mischievous smile comes across Jake's face. It's a smile Jennifer doesn't get to see often, and she understands the reason for it when Jake says, "Technically, Sharb barred us from that building, remember?" he says, his dimples getting bigger with his deepened smile. "And I don't want to disobey direct orders, so I think Captain Sharb will have to lead this paper searching mission." And with that, Jake pulls out his phone, calls his dad, and tells him all they've found, discovered, and what they need.

"It's done," Jake says, hanging up the phone. "My dad is sending a whole team of officers over to Fred's building."

"Including Sharb?" Jennifer asks, her eyes as slanted as her smile.

"Oh, Sharb is leading the team, did I forget to mention that?" Jake says with a smirk. But then his brows furrow as he looks back at the books.

"What is it?" Jennifer asks, wondering what he sees that she doesn't see.

"John was so adamant about how *these* books were his new chance," Jake says, remembering the repeated yelling from earlier. "It wasn't about a will or anything. It was specifically about these books."

"And we know he wanted to replicate them," Jennifer says, referencing the letter Fred sent him denying his request to reprint these copies.

"But why?" Jake runs his hand across his scruff. "Show me this paper-making room of his," Jake says. He grabs one of the editions of *A Christmas Carol* and tucks it under his arm.

Jennifer leads him up the stairs into the main room, which Jake observes and quickly says, "So John was obviously living here, which means his financial situation was not a great one."

"I thought the exact same thing," Jennifer says. And then she takes Jake into the closet-turned-paper-making room.

"Ugh, it stinks in here," Jakes says, eyeing everything Jennifer looked over earlier. He hands her the copy of *A Christmas Carol* as he pokes around the piles of soppy paper on the table and examines the stacks of handmade paper John has in the back of the space.

"That's where the cyanide is," Jennifer says, pointing to the plastic container. "See how it's the same as the ones in Fred's building."

Jake nods, and then -- still crouched down on the ground -- he looks under the table. Pulling up the fabric that's draped over the sides, he sees a wooden box sitting nestled under the table.

"Did you open that?" he asks, pointing to the box.

Jennifer squats down next to Jake. "I didn't even see that," she says. Jake pulls it from under the table, peels off the top, and there -- in beautiful stacks of red, brown, green, purple, and orange leather -- are copies of *A Christmas Carol.*

"You've got to be kidding me," Jennifer says with a sigh. "I never thought I would say this, but I am so sick of this book," she says, ready to toss the copy she's holding out the window.

"Hand me that copy you've got," Jake says, knowing exactly how she feels.

Jennifer hands it over, and Jake meticulously examines the copy from the safe and the green-leather copy he just pulled from the wooden box. They're identical -- same green leather, same worn Pelznickel sticker inside the cover, same gold script for the title, and the same thick pages that are edged in gold.

"Were there more than 14 copies made? Was Alexa wrong?" Jennifer asks. "Does that mean there's more to the message?" But then she sees what Jakes sees. With the books open and placed next to each other, something is off.

The print doesn't match.

The book from the safe has print that is dark black and looks like it jumped off the keys of a typewriter. The book from the box has typing that's crisp and more mechanical-looking. They compare book after book against the one from the safe, and all of them are the same -- identical on the outside but different when it comes to the print.

Except for one.

When Jake opens the red-leather bound book that was at the top of the pile in the box, the printing matches.

"Maybe there were more than fourteen copies made," Jake says, seeing that these books are the exact same, right down to the crooked tail on the letter "g."

Jennifer shakes his head. "John had those books locked in the safe for a reason," she says. "Those have to be the original 14. They're the only ones with number combinations in them. Plus, the 14 originals are all different colors. If I had to guess," Jennifer says, seeing a narrative becoming clear, "I'd say that Robert made a unique, individual version of *A Christmas Carol* for each man who played Santa. He wouldn't have made two red-leather ones."

"So John copied the design right down to the sticker on the inside and the print on the pages," Jake summarizes. "But what I can't understand is why in the world would John want to make copies of this book to look exactly like the editions Robert made?"

And then Jennifer remembers what Alexa said about John: *That man is only interested in money.*

Jennifer takes the replica version of *A Christmas Carol* in her hands and flips to the back page.

"I think I found our answer," she says, turning the back page toward Jake. There in the top corner, written in pencil, is the price of the book: $2500.

Chapter Thirty

Let the Holiday Begin

As far as Jennifer is concerned, this case is closed. It's a clear line that starts with greed and ends in murder.

John wanted to make replicas of the handmade editions of *A Christmas Carol*, that's obvious. And he believed, maybe rightfully so, that he could sell them at an astronomical cost. But, there was something standing in the way of him creating the *perfect* replica -- a replica that no book scholar or trader could question in regard to legitimacy. The thing standing in his way was Fred Gailey and his printing presses.

Therefore, John got rid of Fred, by poisoning him with the cyanide that lives in John's paper-making room. And it's not like Fred didn't know John; it's obvious from the letter that their families had been doing business together for years. So if John offered to come over to Fred's house and make him some pudding and talk business, Fred probably didn't think anything of it. Until the cyanide slipped down his throat.

But, getting rid of Fred didn't make the presses accessible to John, not if Earl -- Fred's SOS partner -- was still in the picture.

Jake and Jennifer know that the printing press building Junior took them to was the headquarters for the SOS, so although they don't have the solid proof yet, they're positive that Fred would have left that buildling to Earl.

So John got rid of Earl to ensure that there was no clear owner of the building. John knows full well how a building can be left to sit -- unattended and ignored -- while legal debates around ownership go back and forth. So that was his chance. His chance to use the printing presses while no one was looking.

"That's why the printing presses were warm when we felt them," Jennifer says to Jake as they close the door to Pelznickels and walk to his car. "After John got rid of Earl, he must have gone to the building and printed the book. Remember when Wendy said she'd been running the store by herself for a few days?"

"A few days is all it took for John to kill those two men and use the presses," Jake says.

"And that's how he got his perfect copy of the book. The book he planned to sell for $2500," Jennifer says, as Jake opens her car door.

"So maybe it wasn't the million dollar department store he was hoping for when his dad died," Jake says, as she slips in the car, "but John was planning to make money in another way."

Jake closes her door and makes his way to the driver's seat.

"I can't believe anyone would spend $2500 on a book," Jennifer says as Jake starts the car, but she knows it's more than possible. With a little bit of research, she found that Chaucer's *Canterbury Tales* first edition sold for over 11 million dollars.

"Rich people," Jennifer thinks, shaking her head.

"Speaking of which," Jake says, looking over at her. "Are we going to this party?"

Jennifer tiredly throws her head against the seat of the car. "Have we done everything we can here?"

"Yes, and Erin said she's sending officers over to tape off the place, get photos, and she's going to have her PD office ship the *A Christmas Carol* books to the Middlebridge precinct."

"And Sharb is checking on the pudding boxes," Jennifer says, not able to stop the smile that comes to her lips when she says this.

"Yep."

"And Junior?" Jennifer asks, tilting her head toward Jake as her eyes and heart soften. "Any word on him," and she feels her heart splinter when she finishes with, "or any word on the dogs?"

"The dogs are all at the police station," Jake says. "My dad said the dogs have actually made the station really calm."

"And Junior?"

"Nothing on Junior. And he didn't answer my calls or texts, but we'll keep trying him."

"He's probably so scared," Jennifer says, shaking her head. "I still can't figure out why Sharb was so set on believing Junior was the murderer."

"Well, his name is cleared now. And we'll keep contacting him until he knows that."

Jennifer feels a boulder lift from her shoulders. "Well then," she says, with her tired eyes and an exhausted voice, "Let the holiday begin."

Chapter Thirty-One

Clinking Glasses of Crystal

They pull into the private parking lot that Jennifer's mom specifically reserves for family and special guests. Jennifer half expects her designated spot to be filled, seeing that it's now almost 9:00 PM, but after Jake punches in the code and turns into the lot, she sees her spot wide open.

She also sees her brother's car, which means he and Julie came in from Wilmette for the party. Jennifer closes her eyes, praying that Julie doesn't ask about the tree skirt, which is still only half finished. But, now that Jennifer no longer has a crime to solve, she can get back to knotting together yarn rather than knotting together clues from murder scenes.

"You think Eleanor is going to be mad?" Jake asks, as he opens the trunk and starts filling their arms with bags of presents, boxes of jam, tins full of cookies, and Jennifer's weekend bag full of clothes, yarn, and craft projects.

"Now what could she get mad about?" Jennifer asks, sarcastically. "I mean, sure we're over two hours late. And, sure, you've got a giant goose egg on your forehead that she'll find atrocious. And, sure, I'll be walking into her fancy party with my hair a mess, my clothes disheveled and smelling like paper pulp, but, I think she'll look on the bright side."

"Which is?" Jake asks.

"At least I'm not taking the bus to Chicago," Jennifer says with a shrug.

They both burst out laughing. And even though Jake's arms are dangling with bags upon bags, he throws them around Jennifer. He loves the carefree attitude Jennifer gets after they solve a crime, and he doesn't kid himself thinking that's not one of the reasons he always comes to her for help with these cases. Yes, she can piece together clues and ideas better than anyone he knows. And he trusts her. Always has. But even beyond that, he knows that she loves to help, and when she does solve the crime, she's blissfully happy.

Jake and Jennifer keep their jovial smiles and light-hearted feelings as they head through the circular door at the front of the building. Unlike Jennifer's mere nine stories, this building has 32 stories, and her mom's penthouse apartment is the entire top floor.

When they get into the lobby, which is covered from floor to ceiling in a cream and gold marble, Jennfer lets out a squeal when she sees Mrs. B, who has run the front desk since Jennifer was a young girl.

"There she is," Mrs. B says, jumping up from behind the desk and running straight to Jennifer. She warms her in a thick hug, and Jennifer loves the way Mrs. B always smells like sunflowers, no matter what time of year it is. She also loves that Mrs. B's hair is still short -- hitting just above her ears -- her arms are still thick, and her brown eyes still sparkle with life. "Your mom said you'd be here hours ago," Mrs. B says.

"Yeah," Jennifer says, "we kind of ran into some trouble."

Mrs. B eyes Jake, who gives her a smile. "I don't know if you remember me," he says.

"You think I'd forget you, Jake?" Mrs. B says, pulling him into a giant hug. "You brought me those bags of cherries from Michigan the spring you visited Jennifer on break. I don't forget a man who brings me cherries."

Jennifer beams up at Jake and loves that a blush comes to his cheeks.

"Although, you had another visitor tonight," Mrs. B says, turning serious eyes onto Jennifer. "Two of them, and they were not here to deliver cherries. More like they were here to deliver trouble."

"I had visitors?" Jennifer asks. She spins through her mental Rolodex of people who might come to see her, but no one even knows she's here yet.

Mrs. B walks back behind the front desk, which is curved and made of gleaming mahogany wood. "Yep. He wouldn't give me his name, nor would the girl who was with him," Mrs. B says, grabbing a sticky note and reading it. "But he had blonde scraggly hair, and he was wearing a black stocking cap. Showed up maybe twenty minutes ago, with two dogs, I might add."

Jennifer almost drops the box of jam she's holding. "Junior," Jennifer says, looking up at Jake. "Did he leave a number or a message or say *anything*?"

"Nope," Mrs. B says, shaking her head. "Came in, asked for you, dodged all my questions, and then he, the girl, and those adorable dogs ran right out of here."

"How would he even know where you lived?" Jake asks.

Jennifer shrugs. She didn't give him this address. "What did the girl look like?"

Mrs. B raises her eyebrows. "She was odd. Didn't talk much. Seemed a bit sad. All I remember is that she had brown hair and round glasses."

Odd. Sad. Brown hair. Round glasses.

"Wendy," Jake and Jennifer say in unison.

"That's how they got the address," Jennifer says. "I gave it to Wendy when we were at the bookstore." And then it all clicks together. Wendy's dad put her in that bookstore because she was dating someone he found unfit. That "unfit" person must be Junior. That's why Wendy was shocked and frightened when Jennifer told her Junior got arrested. And now they're together. And looking for her.

"If they come back, let them up to my mom's place," Jennifer says, not wanting either of them wandering the streets of Chicago at night.

"I can let them up, but you know how your mother feels about animals in her place," Mrs. B says. "And you also know how she feels about tardiness, so you better get up stairs. The party started over an hour ago."

****

When the elevator doors open to Eleanor's penthouse, Jennifer and Jake are almost thrust back from the sounds and sights before them.

There's a four-piece band -- including a piano player, a bass player, a singer, and a man on trombone -- smack in the middle of the main room directly behind the open foyer. More than that, there are people everywhere. The women are dripping in jewelry that accents their shiny dresses, red lips, and sculpted hair. The men are in suits that are perfectly structured around their shoulders and hug their waists in a way that's customized to them. And everyone has a drink, which sparkles through the crystal glasses they're sipping out of.

Every surface -- from the catered food stations to the silver trays filled with champagne that is being served -- is covered in garland, poinsettias, candles, white doves, or small holly berry shrubs.

"Does she do this every year?" Jake asks, leaning into Jennifer. Neither one of them have stepped off the elevator, but that doesn't mean they haven't gotten the stink-eye from people passing by them.

"Every year," Jennifer says.

But she knows this is just the beginning. In the library that's off to the right of the main room will be the decorative Christmas tree -- at least twenty feet tall and perfectly trimmed in lights, ribbons, and coordinated ornaments. And in the sitting parlor to the left of the main room will be their family Christmas tree -- usually standing around nine feet tall and covered in the handmade ornaments Jennifer and her brother, Michael, made throughout the years. That's where they always have Christmas, in front of the large hearth and snuggled on the large, puffy couches that easily seat ten people.

"Oh my goodness," Patrick, Eleanor's assistant, says when he sees Jake and Jennifer standing in the elevator like a pair of scared squirrels. "You are over two hours late," Patrick says, unburdening them of their bags, and looping them around his own body.

Finally, Jake and Jennifer step out of the elevator and into the glowing lights of the foyer, which has white marble floors, gold mirrors on each of the four columns that define the circular space, and a glass table in the middle of the space that has an ice sculpture in the shape of a bell on it.

Yet, by the concerned and somewhat disgusted look on Patrick's face, Jennifer worries that the chandelier dripping with crystals that lights the foyer is really just spotlighting her and Jake's disheveled states.

"My dear," Patrick says with a gasp as he looks at Jake. "What in the world happened to your forehead?"

"It's a long story," Jake says, "But, it would be great if I could get a bandaid to put over it."

"Oh, dear," Patrick says. "That is not a solution. We will get that fixed up in no time." Patrick turns his attention to Jennifer. "Miss Hunter, your dress is hanging in your room, and I don't think I need to stress the urgency of a hasty change."

"Got it," Jennifer says, knowing that even though Patrick is delivering these instructions, it is her mother who's dictating them. And, Patrick," Jennifer says, "please call me Jennifer." Jennifer has known Patrick since she was sixteen, but seeing that a year after they met Jennifer went to college, they've never been close.

"Patrick nods, and then he side-eyes Jake's forehead with worry as he escorts him to his room.

When Jennifer gets to her bedroom, which she hasn't called her bedroom in over seven years, she throws her body down on the fluffy white bed. The silk duvet cover feels cool and relaxing against her, and as Jennifer looks around the rest of her room -- wallpaper covered in hummingbirds, plush cream carpeted floors, Tiffany lamps, and art that looks fitting for a museum -- she wonders if her mom is ever going to change this place.

And then she sees her dress hanging from the white armoire across from her bed. The dress is a deep red color, almost a pomegranate. It's long-sleeved and has a beautiful black satin trim around the high neck and at the ends of the sleeves. Below the dress are a pair of black, sparkling high heels that will make her mother smile and make Jennifer wince in pain after ten minutes of trying to walk in those heels. But, still, they are beautiful.

Remembering Patrick's "urging" for her to hurry, Jennifer takes a sip of the tea that's been left on the beverage cart next to her bed, and she runs to the shower.

Within twenty minutes, she's cleaned, her hair is blown out, her light make-up is on, and she slips into the red dress that fits her perfectly -- hugging her in all the right places and flowing right above her knee. The red velvet of the dress massages her skin, and the shoes aren't quite as uncomfortable as she imagined.

She smoothes the dress, gives her lips another round of gloss, and heads out to the party.

She moves through person after person and couple after couple, barely recognizing anyone. Not that she's upset by this. Her only goal in this moment is to satisfy her growling stomach, seeing as her and Jake haven't eaten anything since breakfast.

Moving toward the carving stations that have overflowing plates of turkey, roast beef, and skirt steak, Jennifer is quickly distracted by the large, shiny silver bowls that are filled with coconut shrimp and crab claws on ice.

Those are two of her favorites, and she closes her eyes as she pops shrimp after shrimp in her mouth followed by as many crab claws as she can fit on the small crystal plates her mom has stacked throughout the food stations.

"Champagne?" a woman she's never seen asks her. The tray the woman is holding has at least a dozen flutes bubbling with golden champagne and each glass has a bright red raspberry or a group of pomegranate seeds at the bottom of it.

"Actually, I'd love a water," Jennifer says, feeling her throat scratch with thirst.

"Sparkling or still?" the woman asks.

"Sparkling would be lovely, thank you," Jennifer says.

The lady nods to a man who is standing next to the table full of cheese, nuts, and different bowls of honey to drizzle on both. The man moves into action, carrying a tray of champagne flutes that are full of clear, rather than golden, liquid.

Within seconds, Jennifer feels the refreshing bubbles of water move down her throat and is ready to turn all of her attention back on the seafood. But then, she sees the dessert station.

The vision of cakes, tarts covered in berries, gourmet cookies, bowls of fruit, chocolate covered strawberries, and truffles hypnotize Jennifer. If there's one thing Jennifer can't resist, it's any type of sweet. When she gets to the dessert station, she feels a grateful warmth move through her when she sees a dozen of the Christmas cookies she made sitting on a plate next to the dark chocolate truffles drizzled with a raspberry sauce.

That's the thing about her mother. She may be surrounded in wealth and sophistication, but she'll never sacrifice her family for it.

"I knew I'd find you with the desserts."

Jennifer's smile grows even bigger when she hears Jake's voice.

She turns around and is almost stunned by the sight of him. His tall body is perfectly trimmed in a navy and white pin-striped suit. The silky navy tie that pops against the crisp white button down shirt he's wearing perfectly matches the navy pocket square he has. And his shoes, a deep brown that shine in the chandelier light above them, are the perfect finish to the suit. And somehow, Patrick has worked his magic on the goose egg Jake had. It's barely noticeable now.

"You knew I'd be by the desserts, huh?" Jennifer says, slyly popping a truffle in her mouth. "You know, you should really be a detective."

Jake lets out a sarcastic chuckle, and then he lets his eyes take in every part of her. A blush comes to his cheeks as he says, "You look really...amazingly beautiful."

"Thanks," Jennifer says. "You think I'll still be beautiful if I shove that entire piece of chocolate cake in my mouth?" she says pointing to a large triangle of cake covered in thick icing.

"Uh, then you'll be gorgeous," Jake says, smiling and also turning his attention to the desserts. "I'm so hungry," he says, but then all of his hunger stops when he sees the cut glass bowl that's at the edge of the dessert table. "Are you kidding me?" Jake says.

"What?" And then Jennifer sees what he sees. It's a giant bowl of pudding. Brown, unappetizing, and will-never-be-the-same pudding.

Jennifer links her arm through Jake's. "On second thought," she says, "let's go to the carving station."

They both turn around, but they don't make it one step. Right in front of them is Eleanor, and although she's surrounded with holiday revelry, she is anything but jolly.

Chapter Thirty-Two

An Interrupted Holiday Mingle

Eleanor's dress is more like a gown. It's fully black, long-sleeved, the hem dusts the ground, and there is a large key hole cut out on the back of the dress. She's wearing her tear drop diamond earrings that match the diamond necklace that shines against the black, matte fabric of her dress. Her blonde hair is pinned up in a simple twist, her lips are a deep red, and there's a sparkle about her that comes out whenever Eleanor is entertaining.

"You look beautiful, darling," Eleanor says, leaning in and kissing Jennifer on the cheek. "I knew that dress would suit you perfectly." And then she turns her eyes to Jake. She scans over his suit, his stance, and his smile. "Looks like you polish up nicely," Eleanor says. "Now if we could only get you two to arrive on time."

"I'm so sorry, mom. We were totally sidetracked at this bookstore, and--"

Eleanor holds up her hand, silencing Jennifer's story. "We'll talk about it tomorrow, when we don't have guests. Plus, you're here now. That's all that matters," Eleanor says. She grabs Jennifer by the hand. "Now, come with me. I want to introduce you to some people."

"Some people" turns into ten, then twenty, and then thirty people. Jennifer isn't sure she can smile anymore, and she keeps catching Jake eyeing the food that their "introductions" keep them separated from.

"Mom, Jake and I really need to eat something. Is there any chance we can take a break from the mingling?"

"Just one more introduction," Eleanor says, untucking Jennifer's hair from behind her ear. "Then I will turn you loose on all the food. Your Christmas cookies look beautiful, by the way," her mom says, giving Jennifer a warm and thankful smile. "You know I love the white trees."

Jennifer sees a glimmer in her mom's eye when she says this. This party, or more importantly, Jennifer being at this party, means a lot to her mother, so Jennifer takes a deep breath and gets ready for the next round of small talk. But before the next introduction can happen, Jennifer's brother, Michael, and her sister-in-law, Julie, are right in front of them. They all exchange hugs, and as soon as Jennifer pulls back from her hug with Julie, the inquisition begins.

How did the tree skirt turn out? Did you finish the baby's stocking? Have you seen the carving stations? Have I told you I've gone vegan; it's so much better for the baby. I'm surprised you didn't wear your hair up. You always look more put together with your hair up. And I hope the jam you made isn't strawberry. Strawberries make me sick now, thanks to this little bundle.

Julie puts her hand on her belly when she says this last sentence, and Jennifer looks at the bump curving out of Julie's black dress that's fully outlined in a silver trim. Although Julie is always pretty -- with her dark black hair that hits right at her shoulder and that she always wears perfectly straight, her athletic body that shows her discipline and strength, and her perfectly sized straight teeth that shine under her big smile -- now that she's six months pregnant, she looks radiant.

Jennifer, although she doesn't want to, feels a tinge of envy. Julie is a year younger than Jennifer; yet, she's already married and with a baby on the way. Jennifer wishes things like that didn't get to her; she knows she has such a great life in Middlebridge, but when she sees Julie lean over and kiss Michael, it uncovers a small emptiness in Jennifer's heart that she didn't know was even there.

"Come, dear," Eleanor says, as if she knows the uncomfortable sadness Jennifer is feeling. Jake must also sense it because he puts his hand on the small of Jennifer's back and smiles down at her while Eleanor weaves them through more people who all say hello, and tell Eleanor what a great party it is this year.

"You just need to say hello to the Morgans," Eleanor says, but Jennifer is no longer listening. Because across the room Jennifer spots a girl in brown clothes and a long, drab down coat that's fully unzipped.

"Wendy," Jennifer whispers to herself, but Jake snaps to attention when he hears that name.

"Where?" he asks. He scans the room and sees Wendy frantically weaving through the guests and sticking out like a moth in a butterfly garden.

"Wendy," Jennifer says, this time her voice at full volume. She doesn't care that her loud voice attracts the attention of those around her or elicits a disapproving look from her mother. All that matters is that Wendy follows the sound of that voice and makes her way straight to Jake and Jennifer.

"They took him," Wendy says, as soon as she gets in front of them. "They took him, and I can't get to him." Her voice is panicked. Her eyes are on the brink of crying. And every part of her is shaking.

"Who took whom?" Jake asks, but Jennifer already knows the answer.

Junior. Someone has taken Junior. Immediately, Jennifer thinks of how scared Junior was when he showed up at Jake's house, like he knew someone was coming after him.

"I...I...don't know who took my dad. It was two men I've never seen before, but he's gone."

"What?" Jennifer asks, not expecting this answer. She reaches out and tries to comfort Wendy, but there's no comforting anyone in a situation like this. "Did they also take Junior?"

Wendy shakes her head. "Junior is downstairs. They wouldn't let him come up with the dogs, and Junior won't separate from the dogs. Not after what happened earlier."

Jennifer's mind races trying to piece everything together. Wendy's dad is missing. No, her dad was taken. Junior is downstairs, having run away from the police, and somehow he has the dogs with them.

"Why would someone take your dad?" Jake asks. His face is coated in concern. He wishes they could go somewhere secluded to talk -- without Eleanor standing next to him or the people from the party listening in. But, this situation is too urgent to interrupt.

Wendy looks up at him, and her voice shakes when she says, "The book." Her chin quivers and her eyes brim with tears. She turns those tear-soaked eyes on Jennifer. "They're after the book I gave Alexa. They think my dad has it." And then she breaks out into full sobs.

None of this makes sense in Jennifer's mind. They have their culprit. John was the one collecting the books, so if he's in police custody, then any concerns about those books should be literally off the shelf.

Unless, Jennifer thinks, feeling her stomach turn over on itself. *Unless they've arrested the wrong man.*

Chapter Thirty-Three

The Pudding Confession

With every cry Wendy lets out, more and more eyes from the party turn on her.

"Honey," Eleanor says, softly putting her hand on Jennifer's back, "perhaps you would like to take your guest to your room. Or somewhere more private."

Jennifer nods at her mom, knowing that she's right. Exposing Wendy to the slanted looks of the guests is not going to help Wendy or her upset state, so Jennifer and Jake lead Wendy out of the party spotlight. But rather than taking Wendy to her bedroom, Jennifer leads them all to the front foyer. She grabs her coat from the side closet and throws Jake his coat before she pushes the elevator button.

"It's all my fault," Wendy cries. "If I hadn't taken that book from my dad, then none of this would be happening." Wendy sniffles, and Jennifer rubs her back. The elevator opens, and the three of them walk into it.

When the elevator closes and the stares and sounds of the party finally disappear, Jennifer feels like she can break her silence.

"How do you know they were after the book?" Jennifer asks.

"I heard them," Wendy says. "They didn't know I was home. I was hiding even before they got there."

Jake and Jennifer both throw Wendy a puzzled look. "Why were you hiding in your own home?" Jake asks.

"Junior had text saying he was coming to Chicago, and I knew my dad wouldn't let me see him because he hates Junior, so I hid in the closet in my dad's study."

Jennifer and Jake's puzzled looks continue. "Why did you hide in the closet in your dad's study?" Jennifer asks.

"There's a fire escape out the window of my dad's study, so that's where I sneak out. But when I was hiding, two men brought my dad in," Wendy says, her eyes growing big with panic as she relives the memory. "They kept saying, 'show us where it's at,' and my dad went to the exact spot where he kept that book. But it wasn't there..." her voice trails off and sobs replace her words. Finally she slips out, "He couldn't find the book because I had taken it last year without him knowing." Her sobs and tears rip out of her. "So they hit him over the head, and then took him."

Jennifer's heart breaks as she sees how guilty and worried Wendy is. She throws her arms around her and tries to soothe her with a strong hug and by telling her it's going to be okay.

"But it's not going to be okay," Wendy cries. "Junior told me what they did to those other men. The other Santas."

Jennifer's eyes shoot up to Jake. "Was your dad a Santa?" Jennifer asks, trying not to let the panic in her voice show too much.

Wendy nods. "He did it as a favor to my grandfather," she says. "The last year Diamonts was open he played Santa." Wendy's tear-soaked eyes look up at Jennifer. "That's why I took the book," Wendy confesses as she looks down at her fidgeting fingers. "He was so upset when Diamonts closed that I didn't want him reminded of those days, and Alexa was always going on and on about how much she wanted one of those books. She's the one that even told me about the editions, so when I gave it to her, I thought it was a win-win."

The elevator doors open, and Jennifer takes Wendy softly by the hand, but she also hastily moves down the corridor toward the front lobby. She wants to get to Junior and find out what he knows. Because he knows something. And for some reason, Sharb thought

Junior was the guilty one, so Jennifer is determined to get some answers.

They get to the lobby, and Jennifer sees that the front desk is empty. Mrs. B is no longer there. Instead, she is squatting down next to the two dogs Junior has at the ends of the leashes he's holding.

"Eb," Jennifer lets out, not able to contain herself when she sees the little golden lab. Although he's sitting calmly right next to the golden retriever, who Mrs. B is petting, Eb jumps into action when he hears Jennifer's voice. He yips and scurries into place trying to get to her.

Running over to him, Jennifer scoops him up in her arms and lets him lick her neck and face. When he's had his fill, and burrowed himself comfortably in her arms, Jennifer turns her eyes on Junior.

"You need to start talking," Jennifer says, her voice surprisingly calm. The only time Jennifer gets stern is when she knows she's been lied to or someone has withheld information from her. She's not sure which one is true when it comes to Junior, but she knows it's one of them. Yet, with Eb in her arms, she feels like love is baking through her, so her sternness doesn't bubble to the surface.

"I'm sorry," Junior says. "I thought I'd be in trouble if I confessed."

"Confessed to what?" Jake asks, but Junior's eyes fall on Mrs. B, who is still petting the golden retriever that has stationed himself right next to Jake's leg again. Whatever Junior wants to say, he doesn't want to say it in front of Mrs. B. "How about we go outside and talk," Jake says.

Mrs. B waves goodbye to the dogs as they all make their way out to the front of the building.

"Okay," Jake says, reaching down and petting the retriever who refuses to leave his side. "Start talking."

"You both know that I burned the Dickens books at Fred's house," Junior says, and then he turns his sight right on Jennifer. "What you don't know is that I was the one who launched the pudding at your windows."

"What?" Jennifer asks, completely shocked.

"There's more," Junior says, hesitantly. "I also filled your parking space with the pudding." Then he turns to Jake, "And I was planting pudding bombs below your windows before you all came and got me."

"I hate pudding," Jake says.

Now Jennifer understands why Sharb thought Junior was at least somewhat guilty for the crimes. Because he *is* guilty for part of the crimes.

"Why would you do that?" Jennifer asks.

"Because I was told that if I didn't, me and my dogs were going to pay for it."

"What do you mean 'your dogs?'" Jake asks. "What's the situation with these dogs?"

"That's what I was trying to tell you when we went to Ebenezer's Home," Junior says, "before the whole cop situation. I was lousy as a Santa, but I seem to have a knack when it comes to dogs," he says, reaching out and petting Eb's head, who rests quietly in Jennifer's arms.

Eb licks Junior's hand and then scurries back over into Junior's arms.

"Fred saw that I bonded with dogs, and he saw how much I loved them and how much they gave back to me." Junior kisses the top of Eb's head. "I wanted to give that love to other people, so Fred and I opened a dog therapy school. We train dogs to be therapy dogs, just like Lucy here," Junior says, nodding at the golden retriever whose big brown eyes are gazing up at Jake. "Fred said Ebenezer's Home would be the headquarters for the dog therapy school, but then he died, and I started getting threats that if I don't stop you and Jake that I'd lose everything."

"Who told you that?" Jennifer asks.

Junior shrugs. "I never met her," Junior says. "But I saw what she did to Fred and Earl, so I knew she wasn't bluffing."

"Her?" Jake asks. "You're sure it was a woman?"

Junior nods.

"It wasn't John Diamont?" Jennifer asks, wanting to make sure Junior is 100 percent positive.

"John?" Wendy asks. "What does my uncle have to do with this?"

"No, I've met John," Junior chimes in. "The person who called me and told me where to pick up the pudding was definitely a woman."

Jake and Jennifer look at one another, and the same fear moves across their faces -- what if the man they thought had *everything* to do with these murders is just a pawn. Or at the very least a smaller player than they imagined.

"I need to go call Erin and update her," Jake says, looking straight at Jennifer. She nods at him, but when Jake tries to walk away and find a quiet spot to call Erin, the golden retriever, Lucy, whimpers and barks at him.

"He wants to stay with you," Junior says, handing Jake the leash. "Actually," Junior says, "Can you take Eb too? He's in training and needs to see how Lucy walks on a leash."

"Why not?" Jake says, more worried than frustrated. He takes both leashes and ventures down the front of the building to make his call.

His back is turned to them, but it's Junior's face Jennifer zooms in on. It's stark white. His eyes grow big, and she can hear that his breath is shaking. When Jennifer looks at Wendy, she sees the same thing. Something has them spooked, but before Jennifer can ask a question or do anything, she feels a *whoosh* come over her, and then she's blinded.

Someone has thrown a piece of soft, red velvet fabric over her head, and they're tightening it around Jennifer's throat.

"No one move or she dies," the voice behind her says. It's a woman's voice, one that Jennifer can't place but she knows she's heard before.

Jennifer wants to yell for Jake. She wants to fight, but then she feels the blunt object against her back. It's a gun. She knows it's a gun. So when the breath of the woman behind her comes right by her ear and says, "Start walking," Jennifer starts walking.

Jennifer can't see a thing except for the red fabric that's covering her face, so her steps wobble. Until finally, she's thrown into a car. Within seconds, her wrists are cuffed together with duct tape and she's strapped into the seat with a seat belt. She hears the whimperings of Wendy and Junior in the back of the car.

There's more than just this woman, Jennifer decides. That's the only explanation for how all three of them are shoved into the same car and bound. If she could only see what was taking place, but this hot, red hood is keeping her blinded.

And then suddenly, the hood comes off. Jennifer feels the cold air hit her face, but before she can open her mouth, there's a large piece of duct tape put right over it. Yet, that doesn't stop Jennifer from mentally saying the name of the woman doing this to her.

Alexa.

300

Chapter Thirty-Four

Here Comes Santa Claus

Alexa doesn't say a word as they pull away. Jennifer keeps looking in the backseat at Junior and Wendy. They have tape around their wrists and across their mouths like she does, and they're also locked in place by their seatbelts. Jennifer tries to give them looks that say, "Don't worry. We're going to be okay," but she can see that they're too scared to believe her.

In fact, Jennifer is too scared to even believe herself.

After a few turns and only about two minutes in the car, Alexa pulls into the parking lot of a warehouse. It's maybe four blocks away from Jennifer's mom's place. The parking lot is empty except for one other car. A black car. With tinted windows. And Jennifer instantly recognizes it. It's the car that tried to run her and Jake off the road; the only difference is that it doesn't have the Pelznickel license plate.

Two men get out of that car, but it's too dark for Jennifer to see who they are. They approach Alexa's side of the car. She points them toward the backseat, and that's where they go while Alexa gets out and moves to the passenger side of the car. When she

opens Jennifer's car door, Jennifer wiggles and fights, not wanting

Alexa to touch her.

But it's of no use. Alexa has the advantage of having two

free hands, so she easily unbuckles Jennifer's seatbelt, grabs her

arms, and yanks her from the car. Alexa is athletic, something

Jennifer noticed when they first met, and Jennifer's vulnerable state

is no match for Alexa's strong one.

"Let's take them inside," Alexa says, and Jennifer's mind

goes on hyper-observation mode as they walk through a side door

of the warehouse.

The walls of the warehouse are all corrugated sheet metal

that is different shades of rusted red and orange. The windows are

sparse, but when they're present they're large and have single-pane

glass in them. There are large stainless steel vats spaced all

throughout the warehouse, and the ceiling is open rafters, but there

are also mechanical arms hanging from the ceiling. At the end of

each of those mechanical arms is a paddle, like the one on

Jennifer's mixer that she uses to make cookies. But it's the smell

that Jennifer observes the most. The place smells like hazelnut and milk with just a small hint of brewed coffee. It smells like Fred Gailey's kitchen. It smells like pudding.

"Well. Well. Well," a voice says from the side. "We finally meet."

Jennifer turns to look at where the voice is coming from, and she can barely believe what she's seeing.

There in front of her stands a man, fully dressed -- from head to toe -- in a Santa suit. And not just any Santa suit. It's the same extravagant suit Jennifer found hanging in Earl's closet.

"What do you think?" the man asks, twirling and then moving close to Jennifer. "They always called me Ebenezer, but I think I make a much better Santa than any of them."

And that's when Jennifer sees the man's face. But it's not his pointed nose or bushy grey eyebrows that catch her notice, it's his cloudy blue eyes. They're so circular that they look like a fish's eyes. She's only seen those eyes one other time before -- on Fred Gailey. That's when Jennifer knows. The man standing in front of her is Fred's brother.

"I can see your wheels turning," the man says, playfully pointing at Jennifer. "You've figured it out, haven't you?" he says with a grinch-like grin. "I love this girl," the man says looking over at two men who are holding Junior and Wendy. "She pieces everything together, even my *slay* of the Santas. You get it?" he says turning his eyes back on Jennifer. He grabs the corner of the duct tape that's across her mouth. "Show how smart you are and tell everyone here who I am." He rips the tape off her mouth.

Jennifer's eyes sting from the pain, but she refuses to whimper. Instead, she looks the man straight in the eyes and says, "You're Fred Gailey's evil brother."

The man claps his hands together and releases a giant laugh. "His 'evil brother,' do you hear this girl?" he says, acting like he's putting on a show. "But you're right, my little detective," he says roughing up her hair. "I am Fred's brother, but seeing as 1. Fred is dead and 2. I hate my brother, I don't want to be associated with him. So you can call me Chris," and then he gestures to his outfit. "You know, like Chris Kringle."

He bursts out laughing at his own joke, but Jennifer is anything but amused. Her brain is on full capacity, trying to link these pieces together while also trying to figure out a way to get her, Wendy, and Junior out of here safely.

"Baby," Alexa says, getting Chris's attention. "Where do you want them?"

Chris looks up at Alexa, but before he answers her, he pulls down his Santa beard, leans over, and kisses her. Alexa kisses him back, but it's not just a simple kiss. It's a kiss of love. Of devotion. And when Chris pulls away and says, "Put them with Bobby," Jennifer sees that Alexa's kiss was also one of obsession. She's under this man's control.

Alexa pushes Jennifer, forcing her to move.

"You don't have to do this," Jennifer says, feeling her fear start to coat all parts of her brain. Alexa pulls Jennifer toward a large stainless steel vat that sits in the middle of the warehouse. The other men follow suit, bringing Junior and Wendy with them. "You could let us go," Jennifer says, hearing the plea in her voice.

"Shut up," Alexa says. "You don't understand."

"It's true," Jennifer frantically says. "I don't understand. Explain it to me." Jennifer isn't asking these things to stall time, she truly doesn't understand how or why Alexa is involved in this. Or how Chris Gailey fits in with the books or Robert Diamont's will. And, most of all, she doesn't understand why Chris Gailey is dressed as Santa.

"You think I want to work in that mole hole of an office all my life?" Alexa says, gripping Jennifer's arm tightly and pulling her in the direction she wants. "Chris is going to get us millions."

Jennifer is about to ask her how, but then they turn the corner. They're behind a steel vat, and that's when Jennifer sees a man taped down to a folding chair with his wrists and mouth also taped.

Who's this? Jennifer thinks.

That's when Jennifer hears Wendy scream, even though it gets trapped in the duct tape covering her mouth. Wendy fights and tries to squirm free from the man holding her. She keeps her eyes on the man in the chair, and Jennifer sees that Wendy wants to go to him. It becomes clear to Jennifer that the man in the chair must be Wendy's father.

Within minutes, all four of them -- Jennifer, Junior, Wendy, and Wendy's dad -- are strapped to their folding chairs and Chris Gailey is standing in front of them like he's on stage.

"Not going to call me Ebenezer behind my back anymore, are you, Bobby?" Chris says, moving right in front of Wendy's dad's face, taunting him. "Now I'm the one who gets to play Santa."

That's when Jennifer sees the cuts on Bobby's arms. Immediately her mind flashes back to Earl, and she knows what will happen next. Chris is going to put pudding in those cuts. The pudding that's laced with cyanide. And Jennifer can't let that happen.

"You look ridiculous," Jennifer yells, needing to distract Chris. And it works. He turns his icy stare on her. He doesn't say a word, but he slowly shuffles over to Jennifer, puts his hands on the sides of her chair and leans in so his face his only inches away from hers.

"Oh, you think I look ridiculous, huh?" Chris says, and then he turns to Alexa. "Love, could you bring me a bowl of pudding?"

And she does. After climbing up the steps that are stationed on the steel vat like a spine, she walks on the catwalk that surrounds the top of the vat. She disappears for a moment, and then Alexa comes down with a large bowl of pudding.

It's official, Jennifer thinks. *I'm in a pudding factory.* Then, the darkest thoughts run through Jennifer's mind. What if that pudding Alexa is carrying has cyanide in it? What if Chris forces her to eat it? What if he forces them all to eat it?

But when Chris takes the pudding from Alexa, he dips his finger in the bowl and licks the pudding right off of it. "You know, I may have been left with this financial dump of a pudding factory while Fred, my lucky-as-can-be dead brother got the lucrative printing presses in our family, but now I'm really starting to like this place. I mean, at least it has snacks." He smiles, but then his smile fades. He looks straight at Jennifer. "You were saying something about me looking ridiculous."

"You do look--" but Jennifer's words stop because Chris throws the entire bowl of pudding in her face. It coats her hair, her eyes, and she can feel it running into her ears.

"Who looks ridiculous now, huh?" Chris says, and she can hear him toss the bowl to the ground.

Jennifer shakes her head like a dog shakes off water. Pudding flies everywhere, but she doesn't care. She focuses her stare on Chris, and she sets her mind to one goal: She needs to get them all out of here and away from this psychopath.

And that's when she sees them.

The vat they're behind is lifted off the ground, and Jennifer is stationed far enough away from it that she can see the floor on the other side. And on that floor are four golden paws, four little yellow paws, and two feet covered in shiny brown shoes.

Jake, Jennifer thinks. *He's here.* She doesn't know how he found them, and she doesn't care because he just tipped the scales.

Jennifer almost smiles as she sees Jake's feet and the dogs' paws move around the vat toward where she and the others are being held hostage, but then she sees a shadow coming up behind Jake's feet. No, Jennifer realizes. It's not a shadow. It's another pair of shoes -- these, though, are black boots, almost like combat boots, and they're slowly and quietly heading straight for Jake.

Chapter Thirty-Five

Into the Pudding Pool

Jennifer knows she only has two options: 1. She can yell out and warn Jake, but that will blow his cover. 2. She can keep quiet, but that means Jake will get attacked. Either way, she loses.

As her mind jumps back and forth, she intently watches the combat boots take another step closer to Jake. They're right behind him now. Jennifer knows she has to make a choice.

Taking in a deep breath she yells, "Watch out," but then she sees the combat boots stop. The person is standing right behind Jake, maybe only a few feet away from him. But then Jake's feet point directly at the combat boots and nothing happens. There's no struggle. No scuffle. And the dogs seem to be perfectly calm.

That can only mean one thing: Whomever is in those boots is working with Jake; they're not out to get him.

Jennifer looks up, seeing that Alexa and Chris are eyeing her like *she's* the crazy one in this situation.

"Watch out," she yells again, "because I'm going to fight back." Jennifer says to cover up her outburst. To make it more convincing, Jennifer thrusts around in her chair, making it bang against the floor.

"Well, I've had just about enough of that," Chris says, and motions for Alexa and the other two men to pay attention. "Start the machine," he says, and the two men and Alexa move over to a wall that has a giant lever on it. One of the men muscles the lever up while Alexa pushes a combination of buttons.

A creaking that sounds like thousands of rusty hinges being opened in unison fills the room, and then the sound of a huge motor echoes through the warehouse. Jennifer sees the floor in front of her shake, and then she sees a section of the floor retract into itself. The floor opens up and below it is a giant pool of pudding.

"This is something I had installed special," Chris says, seeing everyone's eyes bulge in surprise and fear.

"It used to be a water reservoir, you know, in case of fires," Chris says, "but I quickly realized that I didn't care if this place burned to the ground, so I replaced the water with pudding. And now, it's the place I put people I don't ever want to see again, like…" Chris eyes Jennifer, then Junior, then Wendy, and then Wendy's dad, Bobby. "Like, you." Chris points directly at Bobby.

Looking over at Alexa and the two men, who are still stationed by the wall, Chris yells, "Go turn the paddle on." The three of them scurry off to obey his orders.

Jennifer pretends to watch them, but she's really looking for Jake's feet, the combat boots, and the sets of paws. But, they're not there anymore. She looks all around her, but there's no one.

"Wait," Jennifer says as Chris moves over to Bobby, who has sweat pouring down his face and is pleading under the tape that's across his mouth. He also keeps his eyes on Wendy, who has tears running down her face.

"What is it, my little detective?" Chris says, but he doesn't sidetrack his mission. He grabs hold of the back of Bobby's chair and starts dragging him toward the pudding pool. Wendy thrashes in protest, but Chris ignores her.

"You don't have to do this," Jennifer says. She doesn't know what else to say.

"Of course I do," Chris says. "I have to tie up my loose ends if I want to get away with murder. Aren't you supposed to be the smart one?" Chris says eyeing Jennifer and shaking his head at her. But then he pauses. "Although, it doesn't matter what loose end I tie up first. Are you volunteering to go first?" he asks with a crooked smile.

"Yes," Jennifer says. "I want to go first."

Chris immediately releases Bobby. He moves straight over to Jennifer. "Well, then, since this will be your last moments in life, I am going to give you something only Santa can give you."

"And what is that?" Jennifer asks, glaring at him.

"A Christmas wish, of course," Chris says. "Tell me anything that you want, but remember, I never was a real Santa Claus since Robert Diamont didn't find me *suitable,* the old geezer, so I only grant wishes that I want to grant."

Jennifer thinks through all of the things she could ask for. Of course she wants to ask for Junior and Wendy and Bobby to be set free, but she knows Chris will never grant her that. Nor will he grant Jennifer her own freedom. In fact, she's not sure he'll give her anything she wants, but as she looks at his tapping foot and smirky smile, she knows there's one thing he can't resist.

"Tell me how you did this," she says.

Chris raises his eyebrows. "A clever Christmas wish," Chris says. "And one I'm willing to grant."

He comes up right in front of Jennifer, and sits down on the floor. "Story time," he says, putting his elbows on his knees and placing his head in his hands like he's an innocent child. He looks so ridiculous in the large red velvet suit with white puffy cuffs and a santa hat slanted on the side of his head, but he doesn't seem to care in the least. Although, he does rip off his beard before he starts talking.

"I'm going to give you the quick version," Chris says, "because I really want to see you struggle and drown in that pudding pool." He says this last part matter-of-factly. "But, you have been a good girl following the trail of clues I left for you, so…" Chris says, and then he launches into his explanation.

"Number one: See that man Bobby over there?"

Jennifer looks at Bobby who has his back to them because of the way Chris pulled his chair.

"Yes," Jennifer says.

"Well, he and I had a deal. You see, he had his father's will. You know the 'Great and Powerful Will of Robert Diamont,'" Chris says theatrically saying this last part. "But neither Bobby nor I wanted that will to ever see the light of day. I mean, can you believe that Robert Diamont left *everything* to those derelict orphan boys?"

Jennifer looks straight at Junior, who has been so frightened that he hasn't moved a muscle. But by the way he leans toward Chris, she knows he's listening and heard loud and clear that Robert Diamont left his fortune to the Society of Santas.

"Now don't go getting your hopes up," Chris says to Junior. "I plan on putting you in the pudding pool next, and no one is ever going to find the true will of Robert Diamont. And that, my dear," he says, looking back at Jennifer, "is all thanks to you."

"Me? How did I-- " Chris holds his hand up to Jennifer's mouth and muffles her words.

"I'm telling this story, my little detective," he says. "One more interruption and into the pool you go. Understood?"

Jennifer nods.

"I planted all the clues to throw you on a trail that was not easy to follow and was also dead wrong. You know those coveted *A Christmas Carol* books?" Chris asks. "They were fake. Those were Alexa's from when she was a kid. But she and I planted the idea of them being so valuable in Wendy's and John's and then your head," Chris says pointing to Jennifer. "Made the whole thing up about them being gifts from Robert to the Santas."

"What about the code and--"

"Ah, ah, ah. What did I say about interrupting? That's your last warning," Chris says. "The code inside the books was planted by me, so it would lead all of you dummies to the stacks and stacks of pudding printouts I knew were in Fred's building because…" Chris pauses and looks at Jennifer. "Do you want to finish the sentence? I know you want to finish the sentence."

He's taunting her, and Jennifer hates being taunted.

"Okay, pouty, I'll finish the sentence. I knew those stacks were there because Fred is, well was, my *brother*. So now I'm assuming that you informed the police, and they're looking for a will on those pudding printouts. Am I right? Come on, tell me I'm right," Chris says.

"You're right," Jennifer answers him in full monotone.

Chris jumps to his feet and smacks his hands together. "I knew it," he says. "So, you see, I set up everything -- from the license plate with that teacher friend of yours, who is a real dunce by the way," he says behind his hand, "to making Bobby's idiot of a brother, John, believe he could reprint those books and sell them for thousands of dollars each. All to lure you here and have my tracks fully covered."

"But why?"

"Why?" Chris yells. "Let's see, there's the money, there's the power, oh, and there's the money and the power. You see, the will those police officers are going to find leaves Diamonts to me -- the son Robert always wanted as his own. Oh, and just for fun, I have Fred's will in that building as well. You know, the will that leaves all his buildings to me."

"You killed your own brother for a building?" Jennifer says with judgment on every one of her words.

"Ah, ah, ah," Chris says. "Not a building, but *four* buildings. Four buildings that are each worth millions of dollars. And, I didn't kill Fred. I'm not a total monster," Chris says, scoffing at her. "My beautiful accomplice Alexa killed Fred," he says, looking around the warehouse. "Actually, where is she? And, why isn't the paddle on yet?"

As if his words are magic, a cranking sound reverberates throughout the warehouse and one of the arms centers itself above the pudding pool. And then, the paddle on the end of it begins to spin. Faster, And faster. And faster. It doesn't make much sound, but its speed is terrifying.

"Perfect timing," Chris says. "Story time is over." He grabs ahold of the back of Jennifer's chair and starts dragging her straight toward the pudding where he's not only going to dump her and drown her, but he'll put that paddle in and destroy her.

"Wait. Wait," Jennifer yells. She pleads for him to stop. She's run out of logic because all of her reason has been replaced with total and complete fear. All she can do now is beg for her life.

"I wouldn't do that." The voice comes from above them, and Jennifer would recognize it anywhere.

Finally, her chair stops moving. Chris looks up and sees what Jennifer sees. Jake has Alexa at the edge of the catwalk that is at the top of the steel vat, and he's holding her over the side.

"Well, hello, Lieutenant," Chris yells. "I was hoping you would join us." Then he leans down and whispers in Jennifer's ear, "Saves me a trip of having to find him and then kill him."

"Let them go," Jake says, "Or I let Alexa go."

"No you won't," Chris says, keeping his eyes closely on Jake, but Jennifer lets her eyes wander, knowing that she needs to find an escape.

And that's when she sees Erin -- in her black combat boots and police uniform. The dogs are right next to her, and they're all peering around the vat that's next to Junior, Wendy, and Bobby.

"Let them go, Gailey," Jake says.

Chris brushes Jake off with a hand gesture. "I know a bad guy when I see one," Chris says, "because I look at one every day in the mirror. You aren't a bad guy. You won't kill Alexa." And just like that, Chris resumes dragging Jennifer to the pudding.

She's only a few inches away from the edge when Chris stops. He moves from behind the chair to right in front of Jennifer. He puts his hands on the sides of the chair and says, "I want to see your face as you go in."

The panic inside Jennifer breaks open and it feels like glass runs through her veins. Everything on her body is alive with worry.

"Bye, bye, my little detective," Chris says, standing up and placing his foot on the front of Jennifer's chair. With one push, she'll be a goner.

Jennifer closes her eyes and waits to feel the thick, gelatinous substance consume her like quicksand. But when she closes her eyes, she hears something. It's the sound of nails scraping across concrete. The sound of paws running across a hard surface.

She opens her eyes and sees the golden retriever, Lucy, running straight at Chris. And Eb is right behind Lucy.

Chris has his back turned, so before he can give Jennifer her deathly push, Lucy leaps into the side of Chris and knocks him straight into the pool of pudding. The dogs surround the pool and Jennifer can hear the heavy slapping of the pudding that's taking place from Chris's flailing.

"Help," Chris yells. "I can't swim. At least, I can't swim in pudding. Help," he yells, but everyone on this level is taped to a chair. And that's when the paddle starts to descend. Chris looks up, knowing that the paddle is on a censor. The more he moves, the worse this will be, but if he stops moving, he'll drown.

"Please. Someone turn off the switch," he says, still flailing in the goopy pool. He looks out at Junior, Wendy, and Bobby. They're all literally stuck to their chairs. And the paddle is getting closer. Now it's only a few feet above him and the spinning creates a wind that Jennifer feels against the back of her head.

Erin steps out from behind the vat. She runs over to the pudding pool and reaches her hand out to Chris. She squats and in one full motion, she lifts Chris out of the pudding. The paddle stops.

"Oh, thank you," Chris says, about to scramble to his feet, but Erin throws a pair of cuffs on his wrists and kicks his feet out from under him. Chris slams against the ground hard.

"Lucy, Eb," Erin says, and the two dogs circle Chris. "Stand guard," she says. Lucy growls and shows her teeth. Eb watches Lucy and then does the same. "One move, and I let them loose on you," Erin says.

Chris is frozen. Erin pulls her zip ties from the side pocket of her pants, and she zips Chris's ankles together.

"Alexa," Chris yells. "Alexa."

Jake and Alexa appear, and Jake also has the two other men who were accomplices. They're all in cuffs, and suddenly there are red and blue lights streaming through the windows of the warehouse.

"Looks like our back-up just arrived," Jake says to Erin. "Can you zip these three?" he asks, and Erin does just that.

"You okay?" Jake asks, coming over to Jennifer.

"How did you find us?"

Jake rips the tape off that's keeping her trapped to the chair. "I didn't," he says, "they did." He nods to the dogs, who are circling around Chris. "They followed your trail here the whole way."

"Go help the others," Jennifer says, seeing that Junior, Wendy, and Bobby are all shaking and crying in fear.

Jake runs over to the other three and cuts them free. Wendy immediately runs to her dad who throws his arms around her and picks her up in a giant hug.

Junior looks over at Lucy and Eb like a proud father. "Come here, you two," he whistles to them, and both of the dogs put away their growls. Lucy gallops over to Junior, but Eb doesn't. He looks at Jennifer, who still has her wrists bound with tape.

Eb walks over to her and jumps up in her lap. After a quick lick to the face, he puts his teeth on the tape around her wrists and starts chewing. He chews her free, and with those free hands, Jennifer picks up Eb and covers him in kisses.

Chapter Thirty-Six

A Different Sort of Present

No matter how many times she showers, Jennifer can't seem to get the smell or feel of pudding off of her. As she leans into the mirror in her bathroom and applies mascara to the ends of her lashes, the events from last night flash in her memory.

The cops arrived. Alexa, Chris, and their two male accomplices were taken into custody. Jake's dad called, saying that Sharb found the will -- after dozens of hours and hundreds of paper cuts. That's when Jake broke the news to his dad, and Bobby Diamont produced the actual will of Robert Diamont, which he had locked away in his study at home.

And just as Chris said, Robert's will leaves everything, his building and all his money, to the Society of Santas. Fred's will was also found, but it had been found two days ago, by Sharb. He didn't tell Jennifer or Jake that when he went back to investigate Fred's house, he found Fred's will among his books.

That's why Sharb thought Junior was guilty. Junior's fingerprints were on the pudding launcher, Sharb found pudding remnants in Junior's truck, and Fred's will gave Junior a motive.

Sharb thought the next time he'd see Junior, he would behind bars, but seeing as neither Jake nor Jennifer are pressing charges for the pudding vandalism, the next time Sharb sees Junior, it will be when Junior is running the Society of Santas and Ebenezer's Home. And he has a partner to help him. Wendy.

After their near-death experience, Wendy's dad -- who is facing a hefty fine for hiding Robert's will -- really reprioritized his values. He no longer has any issue with Wendy dating Junior.

Just thinking about those events from last night makes Jennifer want to crawl back into bed and sleep until Christmas break is over.

But, there are obligations to see through. Jake is at the Chicago PD office filling out paperwork, and Jennifer is getting ready for tea with her mom, Julie, and her mom's friends. And Jennifer is actually looking forward to a relaxing day of tea sipping and gossip. She needs a break from dead bodies, car chases, and...pudding.

Finishing her mascara, Jennifer checks herself in the mirror. She's wearing the black dress she bought last month -- the halter dress that ties around her neck, hugs her waist, and then fans out at the bottom.

She walks out of her bedroom and into the main room. No one else is out and ready yet, so Jennifer wanders around the room and stops to look at their family Christmas tree. She smiles as she looks at the handmade ornament Michael made in first grade. It's a picture of him, and the "frame" around him is wrapped in red and green yarn. Then there's the ringless bell Jennifer made in kindergarten by cutting out a single section of an egg carton, turning is upside down and fishing a pipe cleaner through it.

The ornaments may be ugly, but they hold the most beautiful memories. Jennifer hopes she's doing the same for her second graders, and that they'll be able to look back at their creations one day when they're her age. Jennifer laughs when she thinks about little Jessica's mom will be getting Jessica's three-legged pipe cleaner reindeer. And she can't even imagine how Trey's parents are going to respond to his cockroach ornament.

Jennifer smiles at the thought, but then she spots her most favorite ornament of all, and it shifts her heart into full nostalgia.

Right in the middle front of the tree is a white rectangle with a red ribbon on top -- tied in a bow and used as the ornament's hanger. There are four fingerprints on the ornament. One for Jennifer. One for Michael, One for Eleanor. And one for Jennifer's dad, Sammy.

Jennifer remembers the night they all made that ornament. Her mom was fawning over getting the Plaster of Paris the perfect consistency before they counted to three and all pressed their fingers into the ornament together.

And here they are. All still together on the tree, dangling over the presents below. And that's when Jennifer sees the present that isn't wrapped like any of the others. All the presents under the tree are in silver and gold wrapping paper, except one. It's wrapped in bright red and white paper with sleighs and santas on it.

Jennifer squints her eyes and sees the tag.

To: Eleanor

From: Jake

Jennifer smiles, realizing that even though they were beyond exhausted last night, Jake took the time to wrap up Eleanor's book for her.

"You know, one of these days I'm going to get an ornament on that tree," Jake says, having come up behind Jennifer.

She spins around when she hears his voice. "Hi," she says, loving when he's here with her in Eleanor's place. Something about Jake's presence always feels like home, no matter where she is. "How'd it go at the station?"

"Paper work is done," Jake says. "And Sharb officially hates me."

Jennifer bites her lower lip. "Is he still really mad about the pudding printouts?"

Jake nods. "But, neither he nor I will be working for the next two days, so that will give him time to forget all about it. That's the good and the bad part of police work," Jake says. "There's always something new to distract you."

"You heading back to Middlebridge now?" Jennifer asks, seeing that he has his bag all packed.

"Yep, got to get back in time for Christmas Eve festivities at the Hollow Home."

"When does your sister get in?"

"Today at three, but she flies out Christmas night, so you're just going to miss her."

"Well, tell her I said hello and tell your whole family I say Merry Christmas," Jennifer says. She opens her arms and Jake picks her up and envelopes her in a hug.

"Judy's for breakfast when you're back on the 26th?" Jake asks.

"It's a date."

Jake keeps her in a hug for a bit longer as he says, "You know I couldn't do this without you, right?"

"I know, but you have to always remember my rule." Jennifer says.

"And what's that?" Jake asks, putting Jennifer down and smiling.

She smoothes out her dress and looks him straight in the eyes.

"I only work holidays," she says with a coy smile.

"'You think I don't know that by now?" Jake says, picking up his bag and throwing it across his shoulder. "You're my one and only Holiday Hunter."

Epilogue

Judy's is busier than ever. Dishes are clanking, people's voices are toppling over one another as they tell about what they did for Christmas, and the sound of bacon sizzling and eggs scrambling hasn't stopped all morning. The Christmas decorations are still out, and Judy will keep them up until New Year's Day like she's always done. But come January 1, the trees and garland come down and the hearts and cupid cut-outs for Valentine's Day go up.

Jennifer stretches as her and Jake get up from their booth. She sees Bradley Pritchard, -- who is still sporting his black fedora hat, but he's changed the feather from red to pink. He must have arrived while she and Jake were eating and deep in conversation about Julie's full on cry fest when Jennifer gave her the baby-to-be's stocking. Jennifer throws Bradley a wave and a sweet smile. He blows a kiss back at her.

"Such a heartbreaker," Jake says, leaving a gracious tip on the table.

"Hardly," Jennifer says as they walk up front, saying goodbye to everyone as they do.

"I don't know," Jake says with a smile, "I think Matt Kealy would have something to say about you being a heartbreaker. I mean, I don't think he'd say you're easy on the eyes, though." Jake bursts out laughing at his own joke, and Jennifer pushes him, making him laugh even harder.

"It's not funny," she says. "I'm going to have to see him when I go back to school." But Jennifer won't let herself think about that. She still has seven more blissful days of break, and she plans to use those days to crochet the fingerless gloves she's been eyeing, eat the leftovers her mom sent her home with, sit in front of her fire, and just relax.

"Uh, hey, my favorites," Judy yells just as Jennifer and Jake are about to walk out the door. They both stop laughing and goofing off and give Judy their full attention. "I think you're both forgetting something."

Jake checks his pocket. He has his wallet. Jennifer checks to make sure she has her purse. They're both wearing their coats, and their booth is empty.

And then Doug Caster, not even interested in the papers he brought in, says, "It's okay. I'll keep her if they don't want her."

Jake and Jennifer look at each other, completely surprised they forgot.

"Come here, Lucy," Jake sweetly yells, and Lucy comes bounding over to him, resting her head right against his leg.

Jennifer bends down and scratches right below Lucy's chin. "We'd never forget you," she says to Lucy, and she feels her heart twist as the thinks about Eb. He was too young to adopt, and Junior says Eb still had a lot of training to go through, but he promised Jennifer that she could visit him any time she wanted.

"You taking Lucy with you to the station?" Jennifer asks, looking up at Jake.

"Actually," he says, making his eyes as big as Lucy's, "I was hoping you could run her to my place. I'm already a bit late."

"Of course," Jennifer says. "I'm happy to."

"You're the best," Jake says. "Call me when you all get there. Just so I know you're safe."

And with that, Jennifer and Lucy walk off and get into Jennifer's newly repaired blue SmartCar. It feels so good to zip around the streets with Lucy next to her that Jennifer takes the long route to Jake's house. When they do get there, Lucy immediately runs in and leaps onto the couch.

"I see you've found your spot," Jennifer says, plopping down in the chair and dialing Jake.

"All good?" he asks when he picks up.

"All good," Jennifer says, but she hears his voice echo. "Where are you?" she asks.

"Um," Jake says, pausing, "I just got to the station."

Jennifer scrunches her eyebrows in confusion. The station has low ceilings and tight walls. There isn't room for a voice to echo.

"Actually, I got to go, but I'll call you later," Jake says. And just like that he hangs up the phone.

"He's being weird," Jennifer says to Lucy. But what Jennifer doesn't know is that Jake is at a station, but not the police station Jennifer thinks he's at.

Jake buzzes through the last of three security doors, and then walks down the grey-tiled hall until he gets to the final door. It's a metal door. Grey. Cold. There's no name or number on it. No marker of any kind. It's the kind of door someone has to know about in order to find.

Jake knocks.

"Come on in," the man's strong voice says from inside.

Jake goes in and sits in his usual chair. Even though he's been in this office hundreds of times, he gets nervous every time he walks in and sits down. The chair behind the desk isn't facing Jake. All he can see is a pair of feet -- which are propped up on the windowsill that's behind the desk -- and stacks upon stacks of files, papers, and books. Most of the files say "confidential" across them.

"So," the man says, swiveling around in his chair and facing Jake, "I hear you solved another one." The man has hazel eyes, salt and pepper hair, and an authoritative demeanor about him. But Jake doesn't notice any of those things. He notices how the man's voice goes up and down throughout his sentences, just like Jennifer's voice does.

"Yes, sir," Jake says.

"You solved it with Jennifer?"

"Yes, sir," Jake says, swallowing what feels like a wad of tissue. Jake's throat has gone completely dry. He hates talking about Jennifer behind her back -- even if it is to praise her and her detective skills.

"And no one got hurt?" The man asks. He leans in toward Jake, and Jake feels a chill move through him.

He holds the man's gaze and says, "You already know, don't you?"

"You mean about the car chase, this Matt Kealy character, and the pudding pool?" The man asks.

"Yes, sir."

"Yes, of course I know about all that," the man says. "Jennifer is my daughter. I make it my duty to know everything that happens to her."

Jake takes a deep breath, and he feels the guilt that lives with him awaken and move through his body. He knows that this is Sammy's way of checking in on Jennifer and being a part of her life, but Jake has been the go-between for ten years now, and he's not sure how much longer he can do it.

But then, Sammy's hazel eyes soften. His authoritative demeanor shatters. He looks earnestly at Jake and says, "How is she doing? How's my girl doing?"

And there's no way Jake can't answer him.

Do you want more of The Jennifer Hunter Holiday Mysteries? Head to kaceygenebooks.com and

sign up for the free short story, "Christmas Eve

Escapade."

Made in the USA
Monee, IL
03 November 2019